Marigold Armitage, elder d...
ber') Harris, was born on an ...RAF station in Lincolnshire.
During World War II she was an ambulance driver and a
despatch rider. After her marriage she went to live in
Ireland (Tipperary and Limerick); while in Ireland she
wrote the novels *A Long Way to Go* and *A Motley to the View*.
Returning to Yorkshire she wrote the play *Angels on Horse-
back*. After many years of hunting, racing and breeding
chasers and whippets, she now lives in the West Country.

A Long Way to Go

AN ANGLO-IRISH
NEAR-TRAGEDY

by

MARIGOLD
ARMITAGE

ROBIN CLARK

First published in paperback by Robin Clark Ltd 1989
A member of the Namara Group
27/29 Goodge Street, London W1P 1FD

First published by Faber & Faber Ltd 1952

British Library Cataloguing in Publication Data
Armitage, Marigold
    A long way to go.
    I. Title
    823'.914 [F]

ISBN 0-86072-120-5

Printed and bound in Great Britain by
Cox & Wyman Ltd, Reading

Chapter One

The mild and milky evening air had, here in the front avenue, under the tall, old trees, a luminous quality. In it, too, was the smell of turf smoke drifting up from the lodge chimney, the smell of old, rotting walls; of rain puddles; of cows ("hay and honeycomb and musk"); and of the mild west wind blowing over blond stubble.

Rooks were straggling through it, gossiping as they went; the long-tailed yearlings grazing on the far side of the patched, once-white rails raised their heads and favoured me with slow, supercilious stares—a fat shorthorn cow also raised her head from the tufty grass, decided that I did not look the sort of person who would bring her in to be milked, and lost interest.

Knockmoree, on this soft February evening, laid its familiar, heavy pull upon my heart, so that I stood still, gazing as foolishly as any cow or yearling, and as I gazed, there, from round the next bend, Gillian appeared, bringing with her a very dirty white greyhound and a visible aura of the Four Hundred.

It was an extraordinary thing about Gillian, how this never left her. I have seen Gillian ferreting—and no one enjoyed ferreting more than Gillian—filthy, with her hair in her eyes, and her face glistening with the soft, driving

9

rain; and still the associations would be of Claridge's and the Four Hundred, of gold and platinum gadgets from Asprey's, of fittings at Lachasse, coffee—chocolate at Bendix, oysters at Wilton's and very dry Martinis at the Ritz bar.

"Lovely, honey, for me to be so glamorous," she had said once, when I told her of this phenomenon.

Now she was dressed, very suitably, in narrow fawn whipcord trousers nearly as dirty as the greyhound, a thick dark sweater, and a very old tweed coat of mine, patched with leather at the elbows—less suitably, she had elected to pin the trousers together where they lacked a button, with a diamond brooch that would have seemed ostentatious at Claridge's, and to drape her round and slender throat in two rows of pearls.

"What is it?" she asked now in her plummy voice, arriving, and lifting what I have heard called her bitchy little cat-face to mine. "Did something concuss you suddenly?"

"Arpège?" I said, sniffing her. "Yes, as a matter of fact, something did. It was the smell of this place."

"I think it's heaven, too. I think your home is heaven, and all your relations just too cosy for words—all except that *meritorious* sister-in-law, God help us. She will keep telling me how to explain to Andrew—I've told her he's just left Eton, but it doesn't seem to mean a thing to her —Goodness, what's that?"

That was the sound of a horse coming down the avenue at a rapid trot that increased to a canter.

"Undoubtedly one of Aunt Emmy's young ones," I told her.

"Aunt Emmy is really my favourite of all. But isn't it

queer how, although she knows *everything* about horses, and she's so terribly good with them, everyone says so; how she's always losing them—but always.'

Aunt Emmy's young horse now appeared round the bend, going in the abandoned manner—head high and turning from side to side, tail cocked straight up into the air—in which young horses do go when they have a notion they are behaving unlawfully. Long white ropes trailed and writhed behind and around it.

"It will break its legs," said Gillian. "All horses' legs are made of glass. Did you know?"

Viewing us, the animal slowed its pace, half-interested, half-alarmed. A few feet away it came to a violent, slithering halt, stretched a handsome head towards us at the end of an exaggeratedly arched neck, and uttered a long, loud, rolling snort through flaring velvet, red nostrils.

"You're very impressive," said Gillian. "But it's silly to pretend to be a rocking-horse. We both know you're not." She walked casually up and took possession of him. "You hold him, sweetie, and I'll just untwist his poor glass legs a little."

"Be careful," I said, doing as I was told. "He may not have been handled much."

"Then he'll just love being handled by me—such a thrill for him, wouldn't you think? Give me your lovely hind toes." The horse did so, calmly. "Actually, he's a she, now I look underneath. Such lovely veins she has, too, on the insides of her legs."

The filly, defeated, dropped her nose heavily on to my shoulder and blew enquiringly down my neck. When she took her nose away a large smear of greenish froth remained on my sober dark grey suit by Lesley and Roberts

11

(so suitable for travelling, for the country, for luncheon at White's—indeed, for almost anything but the front avenue at Knockmoree).

Down this front avenue now, waddling easily like an untroubled penguin out for a constitutional, wreathed in smoke from the cigar that jutted cheerily from her weather-beaten face, four-square in old cord breeches, gumboots, a species of knitted garment and an amber necklace, came my Aunt Emmy.

"Goodness, she *couldn't* have more charm," said Gillian, with entire sincerity.

She was so right, of course. No unpenetrating 'Beauty Page' in *Womancraft*, instructing its novices, would for a second have advocated, or even condoned Aunt Emmy's style of dress or behaviour—possibly a photograph might have been used as a warning. "Never let your husband/fiancé see you at anything less than your best!"

The fact remained. Never can anyone, attempting to charm less, have charmed more. The County Tipperary was strewn with hearts that had been, in their youth, bent and blistered by Aunt Emmy; poulticed, possibly, by other hands, but never entirely the same. For what heart —even if it be an Irish one—can happily survive, whole, being pushed on one side by a mare foaling, a young one coming on nicely, a pony that would lep the height of your hat, a point-to-point winner that may make an Aintree horse?

"Well, now," she cried, reaching us, "aren't you the great couple to hold on to her? I made sure she'd slip up on the road below and ruin herself entirely. What do you think of her now, Anthony, dear?"

"Sure, she has great quality," I said, happily, slipping

into the idiom that the household at Knockmoree threw on and off as they did their gumboots—all of them, that is, except my sister-in-law, Hester, described by Gillian as meritorious. She, I am sure, thought it both odd and common, and could not think why my mother allowed it.

"It's great to have you here now, Anthony—you'll be able to win the Maiden on her at the point-to-point."

"My very dear Aunt! Has she been backed yet?"

"Ah, she'll be as handy as a dog by March," she replied evasively.

Her round face, beneath its uneven bob of greyish-blonde hair, glowed with a gentle delight. Here was her nephew, the great lad, placed so neatly and strategically by Providence in the best position to catch the filly which he would then be able to ride in the Maiden Race. Providence was always giving Aunt Emmy this sort of delightful surprise, which she accepted unquestioningly.

I had not been to Knockmoree for nearly six years, but whether Aunt Emmy thought I had just run down to the post I could not tell. She did not ask now had I a good journey, did I come by plane or boat, had I been sick, where was my luggage, would I like to wash?

Peace lay upon us, as it was apt to lie upon those drawn into the orbit of Aunt Emmy's careless ease. We walked up the avenue with Aunt Emmy driving her young one— the long-reins untwisted from her glass legs—in front of us. The filly peered theatrically from side to side into the rhododendrons and still uttered loud, rolling snorts.

"Ye rat," said Aunt Emmy genially. "No more oats for you at all."

"How did you come to lose her?"

"Ah, she just pulled away from me. She's too gay in herself by half."

I knew exactly the sort of thing that had occurred. I saw Aunt Emmy setting out; the filly, "gay in herself", stepping along ahead, ripe for any mischief; Aunt Emmy pausing to light a cigar, to admire the evening sky, to pull off her gumboot and see what was pricking her foot —draping the long-reins insecurely across her shoulder, or standing on them with one foot while she held her gumboot upside down and shook it. I could see the filly successfully twitching the reins away and making off excitedly—across the field, through the gate that should have been shut, across the yard, into the avenue—only to be finally thwarted.

"Poor honey," said Gillian, who must have been thinking the same. "So frustrating for her. I'm sure she wanted to go to the village and look at the pig's heads in O'Keefe's window."

Matty, the head groom, came censoriously to meet us.

"You have her cot, then, Miss Emmy. Welcome, Mr. Anthony. 'Tis great to see you."

"Why didn't you stop her in the yard, Matty?" Aunt Emmy cleverly turned defence into attack. Matty snorted contemptuously.

"Stop her, is it, and myself beyond in the box stouping the big horse's knee for a thorn, and she skipping away past like a rabbit. Ah, she's as cute as a Christian, that one." He kissed the filly's nose with utter lack of self-consciousness, and led her away, his face smeared, like my suit, with greenish froth. We heard him loudly lecturing her as they passed under the arch into the stable yard.

"That's a great lad," said Aunt Emmy. "You wouldn't find them now."

Now the avenue bore us away to the left, and ran into a gracious, gravelled sweep losing an endless battle against weeds. Here was the old, quiet house, square and secure, with tall, flat windows reflecting the last of the fading winter sun, with chimneys gently smoking, and the front doors set open under their superb fanlight. On the curving flight of shallow smoke-coloured steps, worn thin as knives in the middle by the feet that had passed endlessly up and down them for two centuries, sat my elder brother, Roger, cuddling a glass of whisky.

There is no other way to describe the manner in which he was holding it. The feel of the glass in his hand so obviously brought him the same comfort and assurance that a child, safe for the moment, gives to the mother who holds it. This, perhaps, was not surprising, since my brother Roger had been, was, and always would be, almost continually drunk. He was also the kindest, the gentlest, the most thoughtful and truly selfless person in the world.

"Hullo, now," he called to us, rising heavily and only fairly steadily to his feet. "You're just in time for a lovely drink. Look out, the puppies will murder you."

Two half-grown Labradors had risen with him. "Oh, look!" they shouted in chorus, "people to love! Come on!" So saying, they hurled themselves bodily through the air at us, to faint with love on our chests, scrabbling with heavy, filthy, sharp-toed paws, slavering with enormous tongues, poking wet and bitter-cold noses into our reluctant ears.

"Oh, how revolting you are," said Gillian faintly.

"Down, down," cried Aunt Emmy, in commanding, bell-like tones to which they paid no attention. "*Down*, I say."

A small working terrier, beady-eyed, stood on the top step with his hackles up, and disapproved bitterly of the entire scene. Behind him appeared Hester, also disapproving.

"Why don't you *train* them, Roger?—Hullo, Anthony, how nice to see you. You never sent a wire, did you have a good journey, where's your luggage, you've got you old room, I see Gillian met you."

"Relax," said Roger, "I'll get some drink."

"But why must we all stay out here? It's cold."

"It's perfect, Hester."

It had been, certainly, a moment before.

Now came my mother, with her round, comfortable little body and her pince-nez askew on her round, comfortable, crumpled little face—"like a pansy the least bit frost-bitten", Gillian had written to me.

"Darling Anto—I never imagined you'd be here to-night—how simply lovely." She kissed the air beside my cheeks, gently, holding on to my shoulders and rising on tip-toe. Amongst the turf-smoke, she smelt, faintly and deliciously, of flowers.

Then came Nanny, bustling and rather censorious:

"You've got thin, dear. It's those nasty rations they make you eat. You'll soon feed up here," and then Bridget, flushed and tearful with drama, appearing unbidden from the kitchen:

"Sure, hasn't he a great look of the city on him?"

Roger put a glass helpfully into my hand, but Nanny snatched it away again and disappeared. To my horror she returned bearing another one brimming with thick yellow milk and in her other hand she held a large crust of home-baked bread, spread to a depth of some two inches with beef-dripping, oozing richness.

"There, dear, eat it up now."

"But, Nanny——"

"Do as Nanny says."

Hypnotised, I did so.

"Do you know, it looks simply delicious," said Gillian. "Nanny, do you think——"

Nanny hurried off, beaming.

"Some for me, too," Roger shouted after her. "Can't let the old sweet down," he said. "We can sit on the steps and chew."

"You'll have no appetite for dinner," said Hester, "and the steps are very cold."

I knew she was longing to tell us we would get piles if we sat on them, but she did not like to mention the word.

"We'll get piles," said Gillian, loudly and naughtily.

"I've got them," Roger said, "haven't you?"

"No, certainly not."

"I thought all women got them when they have babies."

"Only very common women."

"Oh."

Hester went huffily back into the house.

"How horrid we are to her," said Roger, remorsefully. "Shall I go and fetch her back?"

"Oh, no, darling, she's as happy as a bee. She loves us. We're always putting her in the right."

We sat on, in the mild air that smelled of the defeat of winter, and ate our bread-and-dripping and shared the milk and Roger's whisky and wondered if we should be sick. My mother had gone happily off murmuring about a delicious dinner.

"She's gone to tease Bridget, with André Simon," said Roger. "She's going to order a ham *soufflé* and beef olives and *beignets de confiture*, and we shall get a delicious potato soup and bloody steaks and pancakes, and everyone will be happy."

"I don't know that I shall be so frightfully happy, after all this dripping."

Below us, on the gravel, the puppies lay in stiff and stark attitudes of utter subjugation to the terrier, who was sniffing intimately and condescendingly at them, swearing under his breath. The puppies' eyes were rolled to heaven and their ears drooped lifelessly. "God send", they said, "that he does not actually nip us. If we lie as still as death, he may forget us soon and go away." They called to us with their rolling eyes. "Help, help!" But we took no notice.

The last bland light was fading from the fields, the rooks settling in the tall old trees, the cows had long before gathered at the gate and been let through into the yard. There was the chink and clatter of buckets from the stables, and muffled, greedy whinnyings.

"I'll see if there's going to be any hot water for your baths," said Roger, and went away, carefully carrying the empty glasses to save Nanny bother.

"Isn't Roger sweet," said Gillian. "He's leaving us alone together."

"Am I sweet?"

"Not *so* sweet."

"Naturally not."

"Had I better kiss you in case you get to feel inferior?"

"Do."

The white greyhound laid its head—the head of a fond and foolish snake—on my knee and gazed with mournful benevolence at our peculiar behaviour.

Chapter Two

I was lying on my bed before dinner, feeling like a cobra digesting a rabbit, and hoping that this feeling might pass off slightly before I had to deal with a bloody steak. Roger, already changed, was standing at my dressing-table trying to make his moustache curl upwards round his finger.

"Blast the thing, it's terribly tricky, it was grand before I had me bath."

Gillian was just having her bath in my bathroom, so she could leave the door ajar and chat. The white greyhound lay across my legs, sneezing piteously, for the room was full of steam and Mary Chess. It was also full of Nanny, who was peering disapprovingly into my suitcases, and collecting what she disapproved of——

"This could do with a mend—and these—you never sent those to the wash regular—and what's more, dear," she said, suddenly rounding on me, "well you know that Mrs. Lodwick should not be in your bathroom."

"Oh, Nanny," called Gillian from the steam. "Don't be so horrid. I hate that bathroom at the end of my passage—there's a ghost in the pipes."

"There's some people as would be more frightened of other things than ghosts," answered Nanny, Sibyl-like.

Thus triumphing she went out, taking with her all my socks and the evening shirt I had worn four times and two tatty vests.

"Isn't Nanny a love," said Roger. "What shall we do when she dies?"

"She won't. They never do."

"Oh yes, they do. They get put in *The Times*—you know—'for eighty-eight years the loved nurse and friend of the Pigwhistle family'. Rather condescending, I always think."

"Now tell me about everything here, Roger. Put me in the picture, as we used to say in the army."

"We'll have your war experiences another time, sweet," called Gillian out of the steam.

"Be quiet, you bitch."

Roger stopped curling his moustache and took what can only be described as a swig at his whisky.

"Well . . . what can I tell you . . . Hubert is having a big drive at mechanising the farm." (Hubert was my eldest brother—married to Hester. He ran the farm and the stud with great efficiency and a little unreliable help from Roger.) "He gets the most wonderful machinery over from England—pieces called Mark V Muckrakers and Allis-Beaker Turnip-lifting Drag-nets. They all stick at North Wall for months, of course, and Hubert has great fights all the time with the Customs about them. Oh, and Hester—of course, you don't know about Hester!"

"What about her?"

"Hester is in an interesting condition. Why is it always called that, do you suppose? You'd think it was more inclined to be *un*interesting."

"Good God!"

I really didn't know why I should have been so surprised. It ought to have seemed perfectly normal, but somehow I had never associated Hester with such an animal enterprise.

"And very tiresome she is, too," called Gillian.

She appeared through the steam, her thick brown hair dulled and draggly, her face plastered with Helena Rubenstein. She was wrapped in something scarlet and silky and had a very wet towel like a muffler round her neck.

"That's my dressing-gown you've got on," said Roger, accusingly.

"Sweet, Nanny stole mine to wash it."

"Gillian is very naughty to Hester," said Roger. "She will tell her about having Andrew—how she was in labour at the Embassy from midnight until four o'clock, and how in the end she had to be forcibly smuggled out on a stretcher in case people should be upset."

"Nobody was the least upset. Nobody knew. I found dancing took my mind right off it."

"No wonder Andrew is so brutally sophisticated."

"Gillian, do go and put on your gorgeous face. I want to talk to Roger."

"How rude. Tell Roger I'll leave his dressing-gown in his room." She trailed out, humming gently to herself.

"Gillian is a love," said Roger. "Are you really going to marry her after all these years?"

"I expect so. Now, go on and tell me things."

"We'd got to Hester."

"Skip Hester. Who's Master this season?"

"Old George Lanier is back again, didn't you know? Such a relief—we didn't at all like that odd woman who had them for a bit. Girl indeed, as Nanny kept saying, and no better than she should be. I never quite know what that means, do you?"

He paused and squinted thoughtfully at the bottom of his empty glass.

"Go on," I said.

"I'll get you a drink first."

"I shan't have time to drink it. Do go on."

"Of course, you know the whole place is swarming with rich refugees from England?"

"I imagined it must be. I kept meeting people in London who were just going to swarm. Either here, or in South Africa. I may say that some were back again even before I left."

"Some don't care for the natives. I tell you who's settled at Peppardstown—Mike and Jane Harrington."

"Mike Harrington—used to be in the Royals?"

"That's the one. Jane was married to Peter Henley, who was revolting to her, and then to Harry Peacock, who she was revolting to, and now she's married Mike, God help him."

"No revulsion anywhere?"

"Apparently not, they both dote on Hunt Balls."

"What other refugees?"

"Oh, God!" His eyes sparkled suddenly. "A most wonderful couple who've bought that place near Glanmel —Banagh Castle. A Colonel and Mrs. Wilbraham. *Wait* till you see, God help us! Very fat and regimental and overflowing all his clothes and with a great twinkle in the eye. Bit of a stage-door johnny in his day, he told me."

"I'm sure he never said that."

"I swear he did. And I think he slipped up a bit at the stage door, because Mrs. Colonel is a real, superannuated chorus girl if I ever saw one—you know—masses of blue hair, kind of scalloped, and a big bust and lots of little lacy mats when you dine at Banagh."

"I can't wait to see."

"You won't have to wait very long, then. There's a meet here tomorrow, see!" He took down the hunt card that someone had put on my dressing-table. "Wednesday, February 10th" it said. "Knockmoree, by invitation."

"Mama thought it would be so nice for you. She's been as busy as anything, bullying Bridget with *Boeuf à la mode*."

"Does she really think that people are going to eat *Boeuf à la mode* at 11 a.m.?"

"She says they won't be able to resist."

"I could resist easily."

"But then you've got Englishman's guts!" He stood up. "I must have a drink now. You'd better get dressed."

He went determinedly, and I rose cautiously to my feet. My Englishman's guts felt as if they were harbouring squirrels. I peered anxiously into the looking-glass. Was I greenish, or was that an effect of the light? I switched on another lamp. Better, but not terribly good. I looked pale and nondescript and rather pig-eyed. Roger had looked ruddy, vivid and blooming. I was a rich and fairly famous playwright and Roger was a penniless drunk. It seemed unfair. I tore off my tie rather pettishly.

A quarter of an hour later we were assembled in the Green Drawing-room. No one knew why the Green Drawing-room owned a distinguishing adjective—no one could possibly have confused it with the small, dark and dirty room across the hall where my father had hidden happily for most of his retired life, and where he had, in the end, died most cosily, surrounded by bits of salmon rods and rook rifles, horse show rosettes, terrible photographs of highly disliked relatives, remnants of Court dress, old spurs, bottles of worm drenches and veterinary cod liver oil, newly-born kittens, old gramophone records and rusty filing-cabinets.

"I really must clear out your father's little room," our mother was always saying, and every day Nanny echoed the threat—"I must have a really good go at Sir Charles's office."

But my father would stand in the doorway in a jungle rage, daring them to enter, puffing great clouds of cigar-smoke at them and occasionally, moved beyond endurance, lunging at them with a rusty sword. Backwards and forwards he would trample, fulminating, over the papers that littered the floor ("I can put me hand on anything I want in a minute").

"Blasted women trying to get in and make a muddle," he would shout. "Never know where anything is once they start tidying. I *won't* have it——" wheeling round on them with the sword.

Occasionally a timid maid would be coerced into creeping in to dust while my father was safely having breakfast —only to rush out again in hysterics when she heard the morning-room door open. He always seemed to have a strange psychic knowledge of any planned attack. If somebody was to be sent in to dust at 5 a.m. there my father would be, gleaming-eyed, lurking triumphantly, having spent the night in his revolting old leather arm-chair. Screams would ring through the house.

"Really, Charles, *must* you terrify the maids so?"

"Don't let them bother me, Sophie, just don't let them bother me. It's all I ask."

25

"One of these days you'll get some fearful illness from that room."

"No, no, me dear. Nobody ever had it from a room yet."

"Don't be revolting, Charles."

It must all have been a reaction from his life in the Diplomatic Service, when he was always being chosen for the most knife-edge and unrewarding posts. "We'll send old Charles Kavanagh"—so smooth and rosy and clubable, so knowledgeable about wines and pictures and racehorses and furniture and oysters, such an *open* face—disguising such a wealth of cold craftiness for use in the service of his country.

To those posts also had gone Nanny, disapproving but faithful, ever-pining for the Broad Walk and the Round Pond and those dear little fountains at the end of the Serpentine. For Nanny the interludes in London were the only true breath of life, and the worshipful company of Nannies who came to Kensington Gardens with their prams, their campstools, their knitting, their neatly-packed tea-baskets full of milk, Marie biscuits, Marmite and tomato sandwiches. They came every afternoon to the Patch, which was just behind the Flower Walk, under two particular chestnut trees and here they sat above the faded June grass where their charges could play-nicely-with-other-children-of-their-own-age-and-not-go-out-of-sight. There they would sit, Nanny Arbuthnot and Nanny Gerard and Nanny Kilhampton—for they had the strongly feudal habit of adopting their employers' surnames—there they sat and clicked away with their knitting needles and chatted the terribly snobbish chat that they adored.

"When I had the Honourable David . . ."

"Ah, but little Lord Lancaster was a real terror in his

bath . . ." (Lord Lancaster still was, although not so publicly).

"Did I ever tell you about Lady Kilhampton's first, poor baby?" and

"I will say this for Mrs. Gerard, she did carry well, even though she didn't seem so keen on the idea at first." (Oh, excellent woman, little did you know how very, very taken aback Mrs. Gerard had been).

Thus the Nannies chatted through the long summer afternoons, while their little charges played—not very nicely and well out of sight—with scruffy, barefoot little boys carrying minnows away from the Round Pond in very dirty jam-jars.

Poor Nanny—disapproving terribly of the French valet in Constantinople, the Chinese nursery-maid in Peking, the water in Mexico City, the milk in Berlin and all under-servants everywhere all the time. And now she was ending her days in Ireland, which held almost more to be disapproved of than any other place; peculiar was the word, really the only word for it; but she could never leave her ladyship now, not after all these years. Nearly forty-five years it had been since Nanny arrived, hot-foot from Mrs. Boucher (willing to travel and had been only in the best nurseries) when my mother, in a momentary panic, had relegated to the kitchen the girl that Bridget had been, looking after Roger in a somewhat hit-or-miss style. For my mother, driving out to tea, had chanced to see Bridget in conversation with the steward's wife, whose small and filthy child lay happily in a state of coma with a jam-smeared comforter protruding from its contented lips. Roger, always a restive child, had been squeaking angrily to himself and Bridget, never ceasing to chat, had casually borrowed the comforter and popped it, unwiped, into Roger's willing mouth. My mother, vague as she was, could not but observe a certain lack of hygienic sense—Bridget was set to wash dishes, and the omnipotent Mrs. Boucher produced Nanny; just then emerging, frilly-capped and starchy-aproned, from the chrysalis of nurserymaid-dom.

And here was Nanny still, withered as a nut, taking all my clothes to wash and saying she didn't suppose I had seen the Peter Pan statue again? Alas, I never had. I am sure that Nanny always thought of my life in London as consisting of playing on the patch and having milk and Marie biscuits for tea—she never visualised me bored and drunk at the Ivy, congratulating and congratulated in dressing-rooms, struggling angrily and helplessly with last acts in my Albany rooms or lunching in aggressive camaraderie with my agent at Claridge's.

Poor Nanny—or was it I who was poor? My London lacked the charm and innocence of hers.

"Snap out of it, sweet," said Gillian. "Is it the dripping?"

She was looking bitchy and supremely beddable in an emerald green house-coat that a kind girl friend had sent her from Hatty Carnegie. She had experimented with Bugle Red on her lips and Angelic Pink on her nails, and they blended remarkably well. A slight undercurrent of Arpège beneath a fresh application of Prétexte did nobody any harm. She made a remarkable foil for Aunt Emmy, who had arranged herself quite normally in a dowager gown of black velvet, but had omitted to remove the knitted garment she had worn all day ("in case would me rheumatism creep on") which now poked up wilfully above her semi-décolletage; do what she would to poke it down.

"I thought me amber would hide it," she explained.

"Never mind, Aunt Emmy, it's madly fashionable, Dior is mixing wool and velvet like anything at this very moment."

Aunt Emmy gave Gillian a blank, uncomprehending stare.

"Whatever does she mean, Anthony?"

"Take no notice, Aunt Emmy, she's showing off. Look, here's Hubert."

Here was Hubert, surging through the doorway, rubbing his hands. Hubert, I had always been certain, looked upon himself as bringing a whiff of fresh air with him wherever he went. What he actually brought, even in a dinner-jacket, was a whiff of manure, and generally a good quantity of what he called honest dirt. Now he was scrubbed and shining from his bath, his scanty hair well smoothed, his voice mellow and cheery.

"Well, well, well, Anthony, we haven't seen *you* for a long time—so sorry I haven't been in before—I was right away down by the river helping the men to work the new Palmer Patented Ditch-digging Grab. A wonderful gadget, really. Does ten men's work. I must show you tomorrow, that is, if you'd be interested."

His tone implied that a dilettante like myself would not really be interested in anything so connected with honest toil as a ditch-digging grab.

"I hear I must congratulate you," I said, rather meanly taking the offensive.

"Oh, *that*!" Hubert shifted uneasily and faintly blushed. "Oh, well, *that*, yes.... Don't count your chickens before they're hatched, y'know." He suddenly decided he had said something rather risqué and lumbered quickly off to pour himself a drink.

"You know," Gillian said into my ear. "Hester is really beautiful. See?"

I looked across to where Hester was boring kind Roger. Gold and blue and pink and white, with a mouth like a hen's behind. Fine if you liked that sort of thing.

"She does good like anything, too," said Gillian.

"Stop being so ingenuous, sweet. You know you'd rather be done bad to by almost anyone else, any day."

"I just like to be fair."

"Nonsense."

A very anxious face beneath a smear of reddish hair now peered round the door at us.

"I have ye soup on the table now," it whispered throatily and vanished.

"Good gracious," I said, "what's that?"

"That's Mr. Thomas Quin, from Dublin," said Roger, deserting Hester in guise of pouring himself a drink. "Hasn't he an original style?"

"Why does he look so scared?"

"He always does. It's agonising. I never dare shout when I want him. I just call co'op, co'op, very softly."

"But what frightened him originally?"

"Heaven knows, pre-natal I should think. You must be very careful not to frighten him more, because nobody can bear it if he goes. We've had in quick succession a drunk, a cattle-thief, a tinker and a very correct second footman from the Arranmore's who made a strong pass at Andrew."

"Where do you suppose my horrid little boy is?" said Gillian.

Andrew appeared at that moment, looking anything but horrid or little. He loomed large and blond in a highly fashionable dinner-jacket with what I thought were revoltingly large lapels. That Hester should imagine that anything would require explanation to Andrew put her down at once as an insensitive, not to say stupid, woman.

"Hullo," he said to me. "How's the Orchid Room?"

"Bestial boy," said Gillian fondly.

"Andrew, dear, you have such lovely hair," said my mother, vaguely comforting. "*Do* come on, everyone."

We came on. The threat about the soup held good. It sat sadly in each place, steaming slightly, but Mr. Thomas Quin had vanished.

"I *keep* telling him *not* to do that," said my mother, fretfully, "and what's more, I very distinctly told Bridget *stuffed eggs*."

Roger winked at me.

I said, "I love potato soup," and attacked it boldly.

"Are you going to hunt tomorrow, Anto, dear?"

"Well . . ." I considered. "Has Aunt Emmy anything that can hardly put one foot in front of another?"

"You could have the oldest work-horse if you like," said Aunt Emmy.

"No, thank you. I've seen his face before when he hears hounds."

"Or there's the little black horse—you wouldn't mind if he threw the least bit of a buck?"

"I should mind very much indeed."

"Or there's the new mare, now, that I got from

Donoghue. Sure, she's a great ride, only for her little habit of not rising at her walls."

"That's a little habit I should find very unattractive," I said coldly.

"Don't be so stuffy, honey," said Gillian. "I go out like anything, all the time—you can't think how less awe-inspiring it is over here. Did I ever tell you how I lost my nerve in England? It was at that fearfully grand Kirby Gate. I was staying with the Beaumonts. Goodness, I shall *never* forget! There we all were—but *pictures*—plaited and polished and starched and ironed and oiled—the horse's toes I mean, not what *you* mean—and about a dozen grooms dabbing endlessly at our horses and pouncing at our boots, and catching madly at us for a final rub every time we tried to escape—simply shattering it was. Then Simon Beaumont came up to me—never shall I forget—he looked quite white—and he said, really very sternly, to me, 'Do you know that *not one*, but *all* of your fly-buttons are undone?' Naturally, my nerve went completely."

"Well I must say. I think it was very careless of you," said Andrew sternly.

Hester smiled patiently. The smile said, "We are all women of the world here, but all the same there are those amongst us who are not amused."

"I lost my nerve, too," said my mother seriously, "but that was *quite* different. I can remember it as if it were yesterday. They'd gone away from Ballinacorty, and there was a stone-faced bank on to a road. When I got to it, there was your father, sitting *in* the road, and his horse slipping and sliding away at full gallop. You know how loose horses always look as if they were going to break their necks the very next minute? I said to him, 'Did you get a fall?' One just does say things like that, somehow. Your father looked at me very testily—his face was absolutely covered with blood, I remember—and he said, 'Don't hang about there asking foolish questions, Sophie —don't you know hounds are running?' Then," said my mother, looking round the table triumphantly, "you'll hardly believe me, but the thought came into my head— quite suddenly—*what if they are?*"

A deep hum of horrified appreciation rose from her audience.

"Oh, Lady Kavanagh," cried Andrew, with his eyes popping out of his head, "what *did* you do?"

"I found a gate," said my mother impressively. "It was wired up, and I had to get off and altogether it took me about ten minutes. When I got on to the road I thought '*Now*, I shall take Charles home.' But he wasn't there. Some interfering person had caught his horse, and he'd gone on." She paused. "But *I* went home. And what's more—", she leaned forward dramatically, "I've never jumped a fence since."

" 'Tis a fright," said Aunt Emmy gloomily. "Now, if you'd come out tomorrow, Sophie, I'd loan you my little grey horse."

"No, thank you, Emmy. I'm perfectly happy in my little green car."

Hubert pounced suddenly on Gillian.

"I was going to tell you last night about the Mark V Muckraker, but I never had the chance."

"Darling Hubert—*so* you were."

Gillian gave him a brilliant smile of acute boredom, and

Hubert wriggled with pleasure, like a hound puppy sighting a biscuit being broken.

"They've got the new six-stroke high combustion engines, you know—absolutely fascinating machines, they are."

"Oh . . . they *must* be."

Across the table I saw myself reflected in a Regency mirror—a pallid and nondescript playwright, spooning up potato soup, at home in the bosom of his family.

Chapter Three

The next morning the voice of Thomas Quin came upon my dreaming mind in dulcet anxiety:

"I have ye tea put by ye."

There was a slight clatter by my right ear, and a sound of swift retreat. I opened my mouth to shout "Orange juice" after him, but checked myself in time, lest it should frighten him too much. I uncovered an eye and saw a squat teapot staring at me and a plate piled very high with digestive biscuits. The fantastic February sun was pouring into the room, gilding the faded wallpaper and highlighting a considerable quantity of dust here and there. My suitcases still sat hopefully about, waiting vainly to be removed. Outside I could hear an amorous cow bawling hideously, a misguided bird twittering excitedly in anticipation of spring, and a general bustle in the stables. There was a wonderful, peaceful sense of sunlit country goings-on, and a smell of bacon frying and I was able to feel that I wouldn't do a damned thing about that last act to-day, even if I *was* under contract to Richmond Kerr— for on a soft morning like this neither Richmond Kerr nor my agents owned my soul; or, at least, they were far enough away for me to pretend that they did not. The Savoy Grill, the Ivy, Shaftesbury Avenue, seemed infinitely remote and unattractive, and I wondered that I could ever have desired them.

I thought of Richmond, probably now lying in his green silk sheets, sipping orange juice, studying his hair line apprehensively in a blond tortoiseshell hand-mirror and perhaps wondering if I was going to produce a winner for him this time. But what Richmond did not know was that the West Tipperary Foxhounds were meeting by invitation at Knockmoree at 11 o'clock, and that I was going out with them, (the decision suddenly was made as I ate my second digestive biscuit) on the worst, even, that Aunt Emmy could provide. Let the little black horse hoist and the roan mare take her walls by the roots—the irresistible, inexplicable madness was on me once again and I knew that when Tommy Dwyer sent his long screech shrilling through the covert, to raise the hair on the back of my neck and hounds came breaking like a wave, there across the ditch at the corner, crying deeply for blood and chilling my spine, I knew that then, with the first bank in front of me, with the age-old gestures of hat-cramming-down and rein-shortening and all that magic moment of wild, nervous excitement and determined physical calm known as "sitting down to ride"—then I should never notice if the little black horse hoisted or not; and if it should be a wall, and I on the roan mare—sure, what matter, wasn't she in need of the lesson?

Thus I reflected recklessly and deliciously, lapped in warmth and strong tea, until Gillian put her head round the door and said:

"Do you realise what the time is, my sybarite?"

She was curiously clad in a sort of hunting undress—her breeches, the offending fly-buttons firmly fastened,

36

one and all, merging into some five inches of nylon-clad leg, and terminating in short, fluffy red socks and fluffier pink slippers. Her collarless hunting shirt was open at the neck, and I suddenly found this very alluring.

This was the moment that Hester chose to enter, with an air of rectitude, but without knocking.

"Anthony, Mother wants to know if you would like breakfast in bed."

And what else? her eye enquired of Gillian. Here you laze, with your scarlet woman, whilst I, an upright wife, pregnant, yet briskly astir, am forced to come upstairs again to make tender enquiries about your breakfast. Thus are the righteous forsaken, said her expression.

"Thank you, Hester," I said meekly. "Say I'll be down in a minute."

Hester stood firmly by the door. Gillian, with equal firmness, sat down on the end of my bed and, pulling an emery board out of her breeches pocket, proceeded to file her nails. After a long, long moment, terrifying with unspoken things, Hester went out, closing the door gently behind her in patient resignation to the power of the prince of this world.

"Gillian," I said, "that was naughty of you, not to say provocative."

"I know. Do you suppose she really thinks we've never yet been to bed together?"

"She doesn't think at all. She knows right from wrong."

"Goodness, that must be so wonderful. . . . But what I wanted to say to you was this, honey—how can we prevent Roger from being plastered before they move off this morning?"

"We can't, let's face it."

"But, poor sweet, Hester will be so horrid to him afterwards. And suppose he falls off?"

"He never does."

"Oh, he's such a poppet—here he is."

"Hullo," said Roger, "I've been sent to see you're not sinning, I think. That is, to ask would you like kidneys or bacon and eggs?"

"Both," said Gillian promptly. "At the moment; I may not, of course, when I actually see them."

"Neither."

"Anthony, you must eat before hunting, you really must."

"I shall eat *Boeuf à la Mode* at 11 o'clock."

"The merest snack, that will be."

"May I sin, too?" said Roger. He sat down beside Gillian. "Now Hester will have her orgy for the day—the fleshly lusts now and drunkenness later." He smiled, but his face was suddenly naked in sadness.

"Were you listening outside the door?" asked Gillian.

"I was *hearing* outside the door."

"Not that *we* mind, sweet, in the very least, you know that, don't you? Only I hate That Hester to score off you."

"Oh, well, we mustn't grudge her her little pleasures."

"But I do, very much."

"*I'm* going to dress," I said. "Will you two encourage Thomas Quin to find my hunting clothes?"

"Tops? Pink coat? Anthony, how superb—I shall never, never be able to think it's you," said Gillian.

"Be careful you don't shame him, then," said Roger. "Keep everything tightly fastened."

While I was shaving I thought about Roger. I was extremely fond of him as, indeed, was everybody who knew him. He was gay and generous and sweet-natured, and as much disabled as any blind man tapping the edges of pavements, or paralytic bound to a wheel-chair. And he was getting worse. Once he had only gone on occasional blinds, and been sober for weeks in between, and now my mother had written sadly to me, he was very seldom sober.

"If it wasn't whisky," my mother had said to me once, "it would be something else." And I knew her to be right. My father had wanted to try sending him for a famous "cure"—"It might cure this," my mother had said, "but, Charles dear, I cannot bear to think where else it might drive him." My father had said something about wanting him to make a success of life, and my mother had looked at him sharply over her pince-nez.

"Charles, you and I profess and call ourselves Christians —when did you ever hear Our Lord advising people to make a success in life?"

Such was my mother's faith, simple, unpretentious, unselfconscious, and wholly unaware of merit. She did as she would be done by, and left the chastening of others to her God. There was always an excuse for the awful things that people did—they were unhappy or very worried, or going to have 'flu, or a baby, and what they wanted was sympathy. Nine times out of ten, of course, she was dead right. And if, at the tenth time, she had come upon that cold and calculating evil that perhaps she could not even imagine existing, still she would have felt the fault to lie in herself, for not understanding.

My mother, in a word, was good. And unlike my sister-in-law, Hester, had none of that alarming and militant urge to *do* good which corrupts like any other desire for power, and leads invariably, by its very nature, to such blood-and-thunder phenomena as suffragettes, wars to end wars, crucifixions, inquisitions and the welfare state.

So she was good to Roger, who was very like her and who certainly needed someone to be good to him in all his personal and vicarious suffering. There is in some people—they are very rare—a capacity for pity that reaches the intensity of a passion and can be as haunting, as wounding, as sickening, and this gift—or lack, perhaps, if you look at it from a different viewpoint—was in Roger. Like Donne he felt himself to be involved in mankind; for him the tolling of the bell held the same terrible significance; he had—he was the only person I was ever to know who had—a strong and genuine sense of sin. For skinny little boys begging pennies, for frightened bullocks slipping on frosty market squares, for rabbits shrieking in traps and dirty old women dying of cancer, he knew himself to be personally responsible—and yet was not strong enough for the responsibility, and had refused to face it—doing injury to his conscience, and developing a great distaste for himself in the process. Fear of self-righteousness must have played a large part in this—the fearful example of Hester ever at his elbow—but still, I think, he always felt he might have made a better effort. "I'm an idle, cowardly sod," he had said to me before I went to the war. "I ought not to bloody live."

"You're an amusing sod," I had said.

"*Amusing*—hell!"

"Well—did you want me to say that you're not what you called yourself?"

He looked at me and smiled. "I did rather—that makes it worse, doesn't it?"

"Yes, it does," I had said. "Whichever way you're going, face up to yourself for Christ's sake—sod or saint, just make up your mind, that's all."

But he never had done just that—not after he had found that enough whisky could make it seem that there was nothing to be faced up to, that everything would be all right on the night, and all the same a hundred years hence, that the gift and burden of compassion could, after all, be refused.

I could remember a day when one of Aunt Emmy's hunter mares gave birth to a dead foal after prolonged and terrible labour and herself died of exhaustion. Afterwards I had found Roger, his head bent, washing his bloody hands in the downstairs lavatory. I had made some idle enquiry and he raised a face of wild misery that frightened me.

"She thought I could do something for her," he said. "And there was nothing I could do—*nothing*."

He had been too drunk to appear that night at dinner, for which I was thankful, for Hubert did nothing but bewail the loss from a financial viewpoint and question the competence of the veterinary surgeon.... "All the same he gets his three guineas, why should he bother? It's nothing to him that the stud fee alone was over three hundred."

"Oh, be quiet now, do Hubert," said Aunt Emmy. "Sure, would we grudge half the fee again to have saved the mare, the time she had of it?" Aunt Emmy was of the same stuff as Roger, but her vulnerability was not so great, she was able to enjoy a second large helping of ox-tail stew. And Roger lived gaily, fecklessly, amorally, and went endlessly to Hunt balls and poker parties and to bed with the girls, and suffered a good deal and sought to destroy himself, and everybody said how amusing he was and would have been very shocked indeed to learn how dangerously close he might have come to holiness.

I was brought back from these reflections by small, flurried sounds that indicated Thomas Quin had found my clothes and was now putting them in my room.

When I came to dress, which I did completely as it was getting late, everything seemed very unfamiliar and just a bit too small. I mangled my stock rather and discovered when I looked at myself that I seemed to be wearing fancy dress.

"Oh, look!" said Gillian, when I entered the morning room. "Playwright into Fox hunter—Lady into Fox is nothing *like* so enthralling, you must admit."

Andrew gave me a sideways look.

"Poor sweet, he was hoping you weren't going to, then he could have borrowed your clothes."

"I've an old pair of jodhpurs would fit him well enough——" began Aunt Emmy.

Andrew quelled her with a glance. I saw his point. When you are sixteen you cannot happily appear in Aunt Emmy's jodhpurs and a pair of gumboots before Mike Harrington, who has not only got a couple of D.S.O.'s, but will probably be wearing a Pytchley collar. How far, far more comfortable is middle-age, when there is no desire and no necessity to live up to anything. If I had known that Andrew wanted to hunt I should have lent him my clothes with delight, for my spurs were biting into the backs of my Achilles tendons and I felt that Aunt Emmy's jodhpurs would have been infinitely more comfortable.

Aunt Emmy herself was clad, as always, in the extreme

of dowdiness. There seemed to be no particular reason why her fairly well cut coat should be of a baffling khaki shade, nor why, having chosen such, it should be set off by breeches of a rich chocolate hue. Her boots could only be described as step-ins, and the brim of her furry and greenish bowler appeared to be held together with stamp-paper in several places. Her amber necklace lurked visibly beneath her limp and greyish stock, and her hair fell in rat-tails around her shining morning face.

"Anthony, dear, I'm giving you my little grey horse."

"Aunt Emmy, you're my very favourite woman— what will you ride yourself?"

" 'Tis high time one of the babies saw hounds."

Aunt Emmy, when she got on to a horse, always looked as if she had been put there to dry. A less elegant exponent of the art of horsemanship would have been hard to find indeed. Yet the fact remained that Aunt Emmy, mounted on her sweating, snorting "babies"; on the ex-chaser that would pull the back teeth out of your head; on the broken-down hurdler that wouldn't mind herself at all; on the pony out of the creamery cart or the horse from the Blazers that would stand up as straight as a candle to St. Anthony—on all of these Aunt Emmy would appear there or thereabouts at the end of a run, with an ambling air, smiling vaguely, wiping her face with the ends of her stock, while elegant transatlantic visitors from the Orange County, Pytchley collars and cavalry instructors wallowed cursing beneath the steep and slippery banks or amongst the painful scattered stones of the dry walls.

"Look," said my mother, "it must be later than we thought. Here's somebody arriving already. Anto, dear, *do* eat something—I must go and see about the coffee."

43

A chestnut horse could be seen far down on the last curve of the avenue by the gates, flashing joyfully in the sun.

"It's Little Daisy," cried Gillian with delight.

Roger bubbled into his coffee.

"Who on earth is Little Daisy?"

"A most colourful woman—very, very D. H. Lawrence —full of blood lust for stallions, you know."

Aunt Emmy looked vague, and Andrew titivated.

"Do remember the presence of the young," said Roger.

"When I was a lower boy——" began Andrew resentfully.

"I want to know about Little Daisy."

"Well, she's called Lady Euphemia Coke—old Barrowdale's very oddest daughter, you know—and she's taken that place that Jimmy Sullivan used to train at, and breeds away there like anything, with a very depressed husband who everybody always thinks is the butler—I did myself, it was *most* embarrassing, actually I believe he was once a jockey. Roger and I went to tea there and we had the most delicious scrambled eggs and sausages at 4 o'clock. It's a lovely house, but only sugar boxes to sit on and the best sanitation reserved entirely for the stallion. There's a most lovely view from the house and when I remarked on it she said 'Yes, I can always see when one of the mares is in season.'"

"I don't believe a word of it."

"Peep out now. Here she comes."

An ageless stable boy went riding past the window perched above the swinging shoulders of the striding chestnut—scrappy, straw-coloured hair, a cigarette end dangling from a reckless mouth, a dirty checked coat and red, capable hands.

44

"Lovely horse," said Roger.

"I must go and see about a box for her," said Aunt Emmy.

Gillian went off to finish dressing. She breathed in my ear as she went:

"Do go and talk to Little Daisy. She'll tell you the most intimate things about stallions."

"I don't know that I want to hear them."

"Come along and be hospitable," said Roger.

In the dining-room Hester was moving restlessly about in suitable tweeds. Somebody had once told her that a woman's touch made all the difference in a room and she had accordingly shifted the Christmas roses from the window-seat to the sideboard, put two oranges in two dishes instead of leaving four in one, hidden an over-ripe banana, thrown the Labrador puppies out of the chairs and rendered Thomas Quin witless by telling him that the coffee-pots were not clean.

"Hester, you must have a drink after all your work," said Roger blandly.

"You know I don't Touch Alcohol at the moment."

I longed to ask her what would happen if she did, but instead I soothingly poured out coffee for us both. Roger gave himself a practically full glass of neat Jameson and looked at it cosily.

"I think you really might wait until somebody arrives."

"Then I wouldn't get a start on them," said Roger reasonably. "Look, Anthony—see the green station wagon—it's the Wilbrahams."

The Wilbrahams and Little Daisy came in together with my mother, all exclaiming how warm it was and how there would be no scent, and what lovely flowers, how do you do it.

"And I don't think you've met my youngest son, Anthony."

"*Heard* of you, o' course," said Colonel Wilbraham.

He had a deep, chuckling voice with an upward lilt in it, a fine, healthy moustache, and a stomach that was just beginning to get the better of his breeches. "Even a chap like me has *heard* of you—theatre not much in my line, o' course—just the stage door on occasions, y'know."

Roger refused to catch my eye.

"Tell you what—weren't you in the Tenth during the last conflict—ever meet a chap called Bardon?"

I said I had.

"Very good chap. Dead now. Great pity. Very pretty wife. Married again, o' course."

I felt a mad desire to say "How splendid" and only just resisted it.

"You must come over and see my sheep. Interested in farming?"

I said I was, very, and reflected how uncommon it was for anyone who lived in the County Tipperary to bother to ask this question. I supposed it was because I was definitely established in Colonel Wilbraham's mind as a sort of Inter-planetary Visitor.

"I've found the way to make money in this damned country." (I saw at once that to the Colonel all countries, all governments, all religions and most regiments except his own would be damned.) "Mutton hams, y'know, mutton hams, that's the ticket—your brother's very interested in my little scheme."

I said I was sure he was, and I would very much like to

come over to Banagh and have it explained to me. Then Hubert came up and the Colonel deserted me at once in order to tell him triumphantly that he was trying out one of the new Rotary Cultivators and how it was a perfectly amazing machine and how Hubert must sell all his ploughs and harrows at once because they would just be a lot of damned junk in a year's time.

Later I heard him telling his wife—statuesque in a curiously Victorian habit—that young Kavanagh hadn't much to say for himself; one of these deep fellers, o' course.

I thought again, fleetingly, of Richmond and praised the Lord for Colonel Wilbraham.

The room was now becoming very full of people drinking port-and-brandy and coffee, cutting lumps of *Boeuf à la Mode*, chewing ham sandwiches and telling each other about the ten-mile point they had had with the Black and Tans on Saturday; and the crucifying fall on the tarmac that Freddy had taken.

"And Poodle was *quite* in hysterics so now I'm *convinced* of it," said a high, disembodied voice. "He really is a dreadful old man, that's the fourth since Christmas to my certain knowledge."

"It's pure Melton, isn't it?" said Gillian. "Do you know, when I came over I really thought it would be all gumboots and corduroy and outdoor girls on three-year-olds and mad priests."

"It really almost was at one time. It's all the refugees who make it so smart."

"Do look at Andrew, isn't he sweet, he's having a bit of a walk-out with Jane Harrington, he's pining for her to come."

Andrew was looking sideways out of the windows while a fattish man stood four-square in front of him and cross-examined him about the Wall Game.

"That's Meyer, the candle king, they bought Ardbeg, you know, and have done it up regardless of expense or other people's feelings. He loves all details of Old Schools."

"Bitchy girl. Look, here's one of your mad priests—Father Carrigan—do you know him?"

I told her the famous tale of Father Carrigan—how he had once, having given up hunting during Lent, been cycling quietly along on his lawful occasions and become mixed up with the hunt when somebody had just had a bad fall and appeared to be *in extremis*; how he had been begged to fly after the field and fetch a doctor who happened to be out, and come back himself. How he had said he would get there quicker on the fallen man's horse, how he had been thrown up, had galloped off and had finished the run on him. The horse's unfortunate owner was said to have been indirectly saved by Father Carrigan, as he was unable to give up the ghost for the terrible anger that was in him and he waiting after the Father for absolution and to see his best horse streeling away across the country and he as lame as a tree from the fall.

" 'Tis Anthony, God help us," announced Father Carrigan, advancing now, his wild eyes gleaming behind his steel-rimmed spectacles, belying his sombre appearance.

"And are you hunting? I have a nice little horse, so, would just suit you. Quart Pot he is, out of an Irish Battle mare—you might easy win a couple of point-to-points with him to the glory of God."

"Father, I'm supposed to be writing."

"Writing, where are ye—'Tis not writing would take the fat off a man and strip his soul the way a horse-race would."

"I need to make some money."

"Now that's the devil's own temptation, the very plainest you could see. Still and all, if you really need to—they say Barney's Choice will be trying at Peppardstown on Thursday."

With which benediction Father Carrigan removed his overwhelming personality towards the *Boeuf à la Mode*, and I saw Andrew suddenly stiffen like a pointer and knew that Mike and Jane had arrived. I was looking forward to seeing Jane and determining whether she or Tipperary would come out victorious; when she came in now I saw at once that she was right in there and punching back hard. Her elegance was unmitigated—her coat just dark enough blue, her stock just not too wide, her breeches cleverly avoiding being pink, her slightly loud waistcoat stopping admirably only just the safe side of flashiness, her endlessly long, perfect legs encased in a thin sheath of glimmering boot. She looked round languidly with her vicious, full-lidded dark eyes and absently stroked her smooth auburn head with a long, white, Revlon-tipped and only slightly wrinkled hand—Jane's enemies said:

"My dear, fifty-five if she's a day."

Her allies said:

"Absolute nonsense, she couldn't be a day over forty, dear, even if you're counting gestation."

Jane had many more allies than enemies—not so much because of any special capacity for friendship, but because to be her acknowledged enemy demanded considerable

49

courage. Jane admitted to thirty-eight. Now she certainly looked no more, poised briefly in the doorway wondering, I felt sure, out of force of habit, if there was anyone here who had been on that ghastly party at Reid's —really Christmas ought to be prohibited in hot climates, or *any* climate, come to that.

Andrew made his eager and inelegant way towards her. "Hullo, Mrs. Harrington."

"Andrew—how lovely to see you again."

"Isn't that really a rather beautiful relationship?" said Gillian.

"It depends on what sort of a relationship you think it is."

"Sometimes I think you are quite, quite soulless," said Gillian. "Oh, look! Here are hounds."

There was a general movement towards the windows. Who can describe the lovely excitement of hounds arriving, the dappled and quartered and shaded bodies flowing together, the white sterns gaily waving, the wise, ugly hunt horses titupping amongst them with pricked ears, the harsh voices, "Limerick, Limerick, have a care now, Limerick boy!" the farm dogs barking themselves into hysteria, the colts galloping high-tailed in the paddock, the brood mares whinnying from behind closed doors?

"Well, good heavens!" I said to Gillian. "Who on earth is *that*?"

"Who?"

"The blonde pretending to be Tommy."

I could hardly believe my eyes. Here was every woman novelist's hunting Ireland come true—a slender figure buttoned rather loosely into Tommy Dwyer's old and stained pink. White-gold curls showing beneath the old velvet cap, blue and shiny with thorn scratches, a face like a baby seal using lipstick for the first time; enormous dark eyes narrowed warningly at Frantic, who was thinking of slipping in through the front door.

"Heaven help me," I said. "Has the theatre turned my brain?"

"Darling, you must have known Caroline?"

"Caroline?"

"Why, George's youngest. Tommy had a fall on Saturday—I suppose he must be laid up. We thought at the time he might have a touch of concussion—obviously Caroline's going to whip in."

Caroline Lanier. . . . The last time I had seen her she had been fair, fat and fifteen, with spots, a bulging waistline, a penetrating and perpetual giggle and an ill-concealed passion for stud-grooms. Well, well, I thought. Brightness falls from the air, queens have died young and fair—but how charming when something happened for once the other way round and a queen blossomed, young and fair, from unpromising ground.

Across the room I saw Aunt Emmy making meaning gestures at me, so I went over to her.

"Anthony dear, would you like to get up on my little grey now? They'll be moving off soon and he's getting a bit tissicky from standing."

I followed her down the mysterious back passages of Knockmoree, which smelt of musk, old wine-bottles and moss, and out into the cobbled yard. Here the West Tipperary Foxhounds, infallibly scenting, as hounds will, somebody who doesn't particularly wish to be jumped at, were jumping very industriously, with jolly smiles, at Nanny, who had brought out a cup of coffee to Caroline, and was now flapping unsuccessfully at Limerick and Frantic, Reveller and Choirboy, and telling them to keep their dirty paws to themselves and away from her clean apron which had only come back from the laundry that morning.

"Although to see it, Miss, I'm sure you'd never think so—what those nuns get up to with my linen you wouldn't credit—it only stands to reason I say, religion is one thing and good soap and water is another. I'm sure they do the best they can, poor things."

To all this Caroline agreed, hunched professionally in her saddle, drinking coffee and rating Reveller half-heartedly.

" 'ware Nanny's apron, you naughty boy."

She had a charming, chuckling voice and a skin that looked creamy even in February sunlight.

But my interest was not held. I had just caught sight of Aunt Emmy's little grey horse, towing one of Matty's underlings round the yard.

"Isn't he a great cut of an Aintree horse, now?" said Aunt Emmy proudly and fondly.

The little grey horse must have been very nearly seventeen hands. He had a lean, mean, raking look about him, great ragged quarters and an outlook like a lion. As he strode he ground thoughtfully at his bit and switched his tail. From time to time, he flung his head suddenly skyward and the boy went up with it, hanging like a tassel in the breeze, and came down heavily, calling upon the saints.

"He is in great heart," said Aunt Emmy happily. "Sure, you couldn't give that fellow enough work."

I felt miserably sure that you couldn't. Whether he

would give me more than enough remained to be seen. As I stood by his shoulder and gathered the single rein preparatory to mounting he snaked his lean head round at me and took a button off my coat with surgical neatness.

" 'Tis just his play," said Aunt Emmy lovingly, slapping him softly on the muzzle with the palm of her hand. "Let me give you a leg now."

As she did so the grey waltzed sideways with disconcerting swiftness, and I came down heavily and in rather an undignified manner in the same spot from which I had started.

"Let ye stand now, ye villain," said the small boy, breathing anxiously and chucking ineffectively at the bit. At the next effort I got to the saddle and remained there, perilously poised, while the horse swung and wavered beneath me like a sailing ship in irons.

"Walk him out down the avenue, now, Anthony dear, until they'd move off. He's weary with standing."

We sidled in a sinister, bit-snatching manner through the archway and on to the gravel sweep in front of the house. Here was a two-horse trailer behind a low and massive Cadillac, and Mike Harrington, looking, in a white duffle-coat with spurred boots showing beneath, exactly like an advertisement for somebody's sherry (the best people drink it in the best places) was superintending the unboxing of his horses. One stood already on the avenue, the other was just descending the ramp, superb and shimmering examples of the horsemaster's art, plaited, rugged, bandaged, tail-guarded, treading like kings, looking about them with an air of conquest.

Matty, with the true Irish zest for giving assistance where no assistance is required, was fiddling with the half-door of the trailer; dangling casually from his free hand was a horse which, from its state of sweat, shagginess and nervous exhaustion I deduced to be Aunt Emmy's mount for the day. The expression on the face of Mike's groom, who could only have come with him from the Royals, was an exquisitely delicate combination of outrage and virtuous pity. But Matty was equal to any expression.

"Sure, couldn't they walk into a show-ring this very minute," I heard him saying admiringly. The face of his *vis-à-vis* relaxed very slightly. Did this fellow, after all, appreciate artistry when he saw it?

"Haven't they terrible condition on them," Matty continued, with a bland and wondering innocence, "for hunting horses."

I moved quietly away down the avenue. But there were thin cries from behind me before I had gone very far and Thomas Quin came scurrying after me, waving a green envelope. The grey horse, objecting, started a movement which I can only describe as galloping very fast without moving forward. Anyone who has ever ridden an overfresh horse will know exactly what I mean.

When I had controlled this sufficiently to take and open the telegram—and this involved considerable physical adroitness because Thomas Quin and the grey horse were highly suspicious of each other's intentions—I found the message to be brief and unanswerable.

"Must see you re last act. Arrive Wednesday. Please meet Dublin airport 2.30. Richmond."

Chapter Four

Gillian, I think, decided later that she first realised that she was in love with Roger that morning of the invitation meet.

"So flushed, the sweet, and so slow, and so fearfully polite to everyone, kind of wavering about in his saddle, and smiling very vaguely at people to show he wasn't going to fall off. So very kind and reassuring of him, I thought that was. And then, Hester was so *very* beastly to him when we got back and he was so polite again, the poppet, I could almost have cried."

Hester had certainly been very beastly, standing in her pinkish tweeds, determinedly taking up most of the fire and preventing us from eating our bacon and eggs in peace, she made a monumental picture of self-righteousness. I had always felt about Hester that, had she been present at the taking of the woman in adultery, there would have been absolutely no modest hesitation about casting the first stone. Now she happily flung heavy and nobbly stones unsparingly at Roger; which meant, also, at my mother and, to a lesser extent, at all of us. Roger stirred his tea violently and rubbed a Labrador stomach with his foot and said nothing and didn't eat as much as he might have done. But I was not put off. On my plate were two fried eggs, beautifully shining with bacon fat, three curly, not-too-crisp rashers and a square of golden-brown fried bread. Also available in quantity was hot soda-bread, yellow, cheesy-tasting farm butter, glutinous strawberry jam and gallons and gallons of steaming tea faintly laced with whisky.

For we had had a hunt, a really rather good hunt, after drawing our own covert and two more blank. Towards three o'clock the sunshine had failed and a light, drifting rain together with a decided increased chilliness in the air had made us debate, waiting outside Kilquin Gorse, the wisdom of remaining out any longer. For the lateness of 3 a.m. at the *Bag of Nails* is as nothing to the lateness of 3 p.m. at Kilquin Gorse on a chilly February afternoon. And then with electrifying suddenness, hounds had opened together like an organ with all its stops out, and George was rather breathlessly doubling his horn, and someone on the far side was screeching like a demon and we all went plunging and mud-scattering round the corner and crash through the gap at the bottom and came out uphill just in time to see hounds driving across the wall at the top as if blown by a high wind; George after them, blowing them away now, and Caroline after him, encouraging the tail hounds with those strange, esoteric cries that I shall always believe, in spite of what the hunting books say, every whipper-in makes up for himself on the spur of the moment.

And so we had gone, pretty fast, for forty-five minutes or so. But I am not proposing to describe the run. One run described in any book or, indeed, any conversation, is quite enough. For to those who have not actually been flayed alive by thorns, plastered with wet mud, banged painfully on the nose by their horse's up-flung head, rubbed raw by an ill-placed button, had their spinal cords twisted when their horse jumped crooked off a bank, continued to gallop, breathless, exhausted and, if they are honest, slightly frightened, unable to see for the rain they have smeared into their eyes with a dirty glove, unable to breathe for the clot of mud flung in their eyes and nostrils from the hoofs of the horse in front—to those, I say, who have not actually taken part in this high glory, something of the resulting elation of spirit is bound to be missing. All the same I shall have my fling later on and describe one hunt—one that was rightly famous and was reported in the *Irish Times*, when Gillian jumped the big double on the point-to-point course with her eyes shut and Mike Harrington, following rather jealously and much too fast, turned a complete somersault and explained when he came round that the horse was more used to double oxers.

But that was to come. For the moment I was hungry, relaxed and, but for Hester's beastliness, happy. Soon, I knew perfectly well, unless I immediately stopped eating and had a very hot bath and a large drink, I should be the prey of indigestion, depression and acute muscular stiffness. So I rather naturally continued to loll by the fire and eat.

"And what did you think of my little grey horse, Anthony?"

Aunt Emmy, looking very much worse than she had looked even that morning, was lovingly sopping up the bacon fat with a crust of bread and drinking tea out of her saucer to take the heat from it.

"He's the perfect hunter, Aunt Emmy. You mustn't waste him racing."

The grey horse had certainly proved himself worthy of the affectionate adjective "little". Belying his appearance and early behaviour, bold, temperate and clever, he had been prepared to spread himself like a steeplechaser or creep and crawl like a cat; stretching out gaily to gallop and coming back to play lovingly with his snaffle as a maiden plays with her glove (though whether Kipling imagined the maiden frothing at the mouth is a moot point).

"All the same I thought he'd give you a great ride in the Hunt Cup—couldn't you just see him and he tipping the double like a Punchestown horse?"

"I could see *him*," I said thoughtfully.

"You, a Kavanagh, and not crazy for a ride?"

"Me a Kavanagh and hating the very idea. The spirit may be willing but the flesh is really not to be relied on, Aunt Emmy dear."

"It's all those late nights. All the same, I might as well just get his certificate. Sure, you could be a giant before March."

*   *   *   *   *

Ah, the mellow and gentle glow of melancholy, not to say self-pity, that can be happily induced by the combination of a large glass of whisky and a deep, hot bath following violent exercise. . . . I had a distinct feeling that the poems flowing so easily behind the barred doors of my brain could really be captured on paper and that if I only had a pen in my hand that troublesome last act would resolve itself clearly and flowingly and wittily; touched with sentiment, yet never sentimental; a masterly distillation of bitter-sweetness—at the same time I had a feeling that if I had not actually jumped the narrow, stone-faced

58

bank on to the road at Clonee, that was merely because the gate happened to provide the quickest way out. So I luxuriated, rolling the Jameson round my tongue, steeped in heat and steam and the fearful smell of the Pine Essence that Roger had very kindly poured in for me, ignoring my protests.

" 'Twill take the stiffness from you. God knows 'tis a pity I couldn't do the same for Hester. Isn't it a wonder she could ever unbend enough to conceive?"

Outside it was now dark and chilly and raining hard, which made my position even more delightful. I turned the tap with my toe and let fresh hot water trickle deliciously around me. A large towel waited for me on the hot rails. I silently blessed the memory of my father, who had said:

"Damn it, I *will* be comfortable. The amount of people in Ireland who are unnecessarily cold and uncomfortable is quite astonishing. Nobody can be civilised who isn't warm. Damn it all—*Eskimos* are warm."

My mother had said that she always heard that Eskimos did very peculiar things with their wives.

Undeterred, my father had torn down and pulled up, had plastered bathrooms lavishly on to bedrooms, and installed an oil-burning central heating system that really heated, centrally, and burningly. "And then, of course, we had to pretend to be ill all the time, every winter, so we could stay in our own house and never, never dine out. Otherwise we caught the most dreadful chills, because even if you wear woollies under a wool dinner-dress there's still not much you can do about the feet. But, of course, *now* there are lots of warm houses, because of the refugees."

Very seldom indeed in history can refugees have been invariably associated with centrally-heated houses; yet so it was in Southern Ireland at this time, with the refugees from super-tax, State medicine, milk marketing board returns, and General Interference flooding the land, lending their glorious be-collared presences to the hunts, being done by friendly cattle-dealers and varying between intense adoration and extreme dislike of the native's belief in magic, unscientific farming, dirt, funerals and the Pope.

Towards their machinations, their curious habits and inconvenient pilgrimages at odd hours; their strong sense of mysticism and almost equally strong lack of moral sense; their great interest in, and appreciation of death; their horror of doing any job thoroughly; their extreme suspicion of anything tending towards efficiency or hygiene; their generally disgraceful appearance and behaviour and their undeniable charm, the refugees tended to react very differently, according to temperament. These reactions varied from "You'd almost think the damned fellers were *foreigners*" (Colonel Wilbraham) and "I'm never quite sure if their heads are clean" (Hester—and she had a right, as they say, to worry), through Mike Harrington's slightly more perceptive "The thing is, they're just like the wops —if you treat them as if they were English you're bound to be let down" to Gillian's uncritical delight, "They're so *restful*, you must admit."

And so, of course, they were. Much too restful, too undermining of the restless twentieth-century mind's awareness of the pressing need for perpetual motion at all costs and financial success if possible into the bargain. Bath-philosophy is always gratifying to the ego, particularly if accompanied by whisky and a state of pleasant physical exhaustion. I noticed suddenly that for the first time since—when the hell?—oh, way back—certainly since long before the second war to end war—the burden of the urgent need to hurry seemed to have lifted a little. It was pleasant beyond words. I had hurried and hurried and sought madly here and there—and for what? For bloody-well what? I apostrophized myself angrily, reaching vaguely for the soap, failing to get a hold on it and letting it go again—the four-fold path; the grave; the moment of truth; love at first sight; a winner at 33–1? How was it possible to know? I probably never would know now, that was the hell of it—if, at thirty-eight, I could moon in a hot bath, half-drunk, and imagine I was thinking beautifully and profoundly. Much better to go to sleep, to close my eyes and give myself up to the combination of heat and whisky humming in my head . . .

But they came before me then, the loved and lost ones, the possessed and despoiled, the explored and exploring— their bright vixen faces seen across candles, seen shining with sun and olive oil, seen with painted, parted mouths, half-seen in moonlight, seen not at all but traced with a delicate finger in the dark; all so exciting; so promising; all gone; leaving behind them a faint feeling of thankfulness and not, even, very much of that.

Much, much better to go to sleep.

"Darling," said a voice, "I've seen a hen look just like that. She was laying an egg at the time."

Gillian was sitting on the edge of the bath, looming through the steam and dropping cigarette ash on my chest.

"Go away," I said muzzily. "I *am* laying an egg. A beauty."

"You're plastered," said Gillian, peering closely at me.

"I came to tell you that everyone else is downstairs, dressed and in their right minds, and about to drink soup. Your Mama says *minestrone*, but actually it's a type of liquid Irish stew."

"And to think I was just working out that I needn't hurry."

"You *are* drunk, let's face it."

"Not at all. Relaxed."

"*Very* relaxed, if I may say so."

"Tell my dear Mama I'm very sorry and will she start? I'll miss the soup. It gives me wind."

It was as I was drying myself that another face came before my mind, the face of a baby seal, creamy and slightly surprised, unspoilt, unknown and still, perhaps, exciting.

The next time I saw Caroline was the following afternoon, when we were both standing in the owners' and trainers' stand at Peppardstown Park races (to become an owner and trainer you paid half-a-crown for a little pink label which you attached deceitfully to yourself), cowering slightly away from the rain driving across the course and watching Conor Molloy win a novice steeplechase on a horse belonging to 'old' George Lanier, Caroline's father. I had always disliked Conor Molloy; but now, because he won so cleverly and looked so handsome and self-assured, and so like a film-star pretending to win a novice steeplechase, I disliked him more. An unidentified voice in the bar, as I had struggled to procure drink for Gillian, had said somewhere in the vicinity of my left ear:

"And when are Conor and Caroline getting married?"

And although another voice, female, and slightly more discreet, had replied that old George wasn't fearfully keen on the idea—now, would you be, yourself?—I was disgruntled—quite unreasonably annoyed and cast down, considering that I was going to marry Mrs. Lodwick, who occupied my bathroom in defiance of Nanny, and had occupied more intimate places in her time. I must have appeared very gloomy because my mother asked did I think I was getting 'flu? If so, should she nip me home quickly in the van?

This was a very noble offer, because my mother adored race meetings. She sat happily in the tea tent, eating a succession of revolting pink sugar cakes and dry ham sandwiches while she spun an endless cocoon of fresh gossip, weaving in threads from Limerick and Cork, Dublin and Kerry, as one by one the participants came and sat with her and told her in hushed voices exactly what Poodle had said and Freddy had done ("and he can't be a day under sixty, which seems to make it worse, almost"). To all of which my mother would give mild and soothing replies:

"That family were always wild," or,

"What can you expect, so young and with all that money!"

If no one came to the tea tent she would make a sortie into the bar and round them up like a small, worrying sheep dog. Even those busy with their bookmakers were never quite safe—my mother had been known to pop out suddenly with offers of cups of tea to horrified hardened gamblers like Mike and Jane Harrington—who, losing their chance of getting even money—when they looked again it was odds on—went meekly and had a cup of tea which they hated and told my mother how J. J. Connors had pulled old Dicky's horse in the bumpers at Naas, and how old Dicky had put on a fine show of being angry with J. J. Connors, but Martin had told Poodle that he (old Dicky) was in it as deep as any.

"Well now, the poor old man," my mother would say. "Imagine him doing a thing like that—he must be very hard up. It's all those servants."

I idled rather sulkily by the winners' enclosure, looking for Gillian, and staring resentfully at Conor Molloy when he appeared, sitting easily and, it appeared to me, rather arrogantly, on the big, sweating horse, with his whip tucked under an arm and his reins balanced by the buckle on a casual finger-tip, looking down and smiling at Caroline, who walked by his side, touching the horse's shoulder. I had a sudden fleeting glimpse of myself seated in just such a kingly style on Aunt Emmy's little grey horse, wending my conquering way to unsaddle after the Hunt Cup—a vision which I dismissed firmly and instantly. If Conor Molloy was to be shown his place it must be in some other field . . .

"God help us, you look gloomy," said Roger, materialising suddenly with Gillian. "I won big money on Conor, didn't you?"

"I didn't know you left the bar long enough to do anything," I said, rather sourly.

Roger ignored this.

"Hullo, Caroline, how exciting—won't your father be pleased? Come and watch the next one with us—Willy says Barney's Choice will trot up."

"Well, he won't," said Caroline, "because he isn't going, Roger." Her voice was still rather deep, amused and altogether pleasing. She still looked like a baby seal, even in a beret. She wore a close-fitting tan-coloured coat with a silk scarf round her neck. I noticed now a faint flourish of freckles across her cheekbones, and the way her white-gold hair grew down in a very definite widow's peak on her forehead. I wondered if she had been to bed with Conor, and decided on the whole, probably not.

He had now disappeared to weigh in, and we all stood around the smoking horse and told George he was a great cut of a 'chaser and there was no beating the Cottage blood and would he have a crack at the Gold Cup next year? Then someone came out and nodded to the lad, who took the horse away and we all drifted towards the bar, as a harsh voice started reciting over the broadcasting system the runners and riders for the next race.

"You see, I told you Barney's Choice wasn't going," said Caroline to Roger.

She had very nice legs and low-heeled tan calf moccasins —probably from Delman's, I thought, walking consideringly behind her. Old George must have sent her a long way from Tipperary after she had left school, I decided. I wondered where she had been and what she had done.

"Number nineteen, Mr. C. Molloy," said the voice.

"I'd adore to be a jockey, wouldn't you?" said Gillian. "Imagine slipping out of a little pink number with gold cross-belts and quickly into a scarlet one with green sleeves—the bliss!"

"None of them fitting you and all very dirty and all worn before by endless other jockeys who had sweated into them." I said.

"Darling, you are *not* gay," said Gillian.

Caroline looked at me respectfully. I had a sudden hope that she found such disenchantment attractive and that I might be in her eyes rather excitingly world-weary—a type in a Somerset Maugham story, quiet and cynical, with a muscle in the jaw twitching occasionally, a crooked smile and a fund of rather sinister little anecdotes about human nature.

"Would you mind very much", said Caroline with grave politeness, to Gillian, "if I don't come and have a drink just now? I do rather want to see these in the paddock."

"I'll come with you," I said. "Leave the soaks."

Roger gave me a wordless look and gently offered me his copy of *Chaseform*, which I took rather coldly and Caroline and I set off on that type of barging match indigenous to all race meetings—colliding with people hurrying to the Tote and from the bookmakers; out of the bar and back to the paddock; and elbowing our way through obstructive groups who were marking their cards, gossiping or wondering if there was time to go to the lavatory.

I saw Lady Euphemia Coke talking to Colonel Wilbraham, who was looking distinctly nervous. She was wearing a tweed skirt very much sat out behind and this, curiously enough, enormously increased her masculinity—she looked exactly like a man pretending to be a woman, whereas before she had merely looked like a woman pretending to be a man. I pointed this out to Caroline, who agreed with a charming chuckle, and an exhortation not to be unkind.

"She's really terribly nice, you've no idea, don't go putting her in a play, she'd be very hurt."

I said that people always accused me of putting them in plays—just as if I was making a cake with currants in it—but actually very few of them were either complicated or simple enough to be put into a play like a currant; generally one had to mingle them a bit.

"So you do put them in, in a way?"

I said how could you avoid it? And Caroline said she had always thought that Mrs. Meredith was meant to be my Aunt Emmy.

"I enjoyed that, although I was far too young to understand it, it wasn't until years later that I realised what it was about."

"You do realise now?"

Caroline told me again not to be unkind, and advised me to look at the horses, who were wending their elegant ways around the muddy paddock track and behaving, I thought, much in the same way that human beings might have behaved under the same circumstances; some showing off enormously, plainly enjoying their plaited manes and tails and the occasion for the best coloured quarter sheet, the white leading rein, and the dark blue bandages; some bored; some self-conscious and shy, with hanging heads and sideways glances; some fussing madly, sweating and tugging and ignoring the muttered curses from their lads—I could almost hear these latter ones complaining— "My girths are much too tight and I know I shall spread a plate and I hate this jockey and somebody's bound to cross me at the open ditch—oh *how* I wish I could work on a farm."

"Conor's riding Dicky's horse, Number four—he's fast but a very chancy jumper," said Caroline.

"Are you going to marry Conor?" I asked idly, leaning on the white rail, smelling the familiar steeplechasing smell of trodden grass and hot horses and wet clothing.

67

Caroline went bright pink immediately, in a most charmingly uncontrolled manner, and said:

"Look, the jockeys were getting up, we ought to get back to the stand if we wanted to see them go down. Who could possibly have said such a thing, please not to repeat it to anyone."

I wandered off to the bookmakers and had a large bet, and then into the bar for a large whisky. When I came out again and picked up the threads I found that the horse I had backed had fallen at the first fence, and that old Dicky's horse, piloted by Conor, had won in a canter—word had already gone round that this was the getting-out stakes for old Dicky, and he would now go as straight as ever until he was penniless again—I also found that Gillian and Roger and myself had been trapped by old Mr. Brendan Molloy, who was Conor's highly successful father (he had modernised a castle after doing something slightly shady in timber and sent Conor to Oxford after running an air-line for a year or two and then suddenly ceasing to run it), into going back with them to drink and eat too much and play too much poker for too much money. ("A glass of wine and a chop and a friendly game of cards," said old Mr. Brendan Molloy, who had too much money already.)

Chapter Five

"The thing about God is this," said Roger.

Gillian and I waited expectantly.

"He's going to say something very important," said Gillian.

"I know," I said.

Somewhere beyond the extraordinary sensation of Atlantic tides ebbing and flowing in my head, a clock struck, rather curiously.

"Why would it be six o'clock?" Gillian hissed.

"Why are you whispering?"

"Not to interrupt Roger, of course."

"It's the way you are that matters," said Roger. "Like Ernest Hemingway. You shouldn't ever bother about anything else. People get distracted—I mean, they distract you."

"You're dead right, darling," said Gillian, earnestly. "You'd think it was easy, wouldn't you? He's dead right, sweet," she said to me, with tears in her eyes.

"I know," I said, equally moved.

"If a lot more people didn't bother it wouldn't matter," said Roger.

"Can you understand that, sweet?" asked Gillian, rather pompously.

"Of course I can," I said.

"I mean there wouldn't be wars," said Roger.

"Ah, but there would, Roger, because of our animal instincts—look at stoats."

"That's different," Roger said shortly. "That's love."

"It's the same thing, you said so yourself. It's all terribly unfair."

In spite of an exceptionally high tide which had buried my brain at this moment, it did not seem to me that their argument, whatever it might be, was noticeably close-knit. I began to tell them so.

"But what I want to know," said Gillian suddenly, very loudly, "is *why is it six o'clock?*"

"Time for a drink," said Roger, with a great air of logic.

"I think I had one," said Gillian doubtfully.

"When?"

"I don't know. But it tastes."

"You need something to take the taste away, then."

"No, I don't. I don't want anything—I don't think I feel very well."

"Lie down, darling," I said, solicitously.

"I thought I was lying down?"

"She *is* lying down. Don't tease her, Anthony."

"Listen, is this woman yours or mine?"

"The power urge," said Roger censoriously. "It's a fear-fully wicked thing. Like that man said. He knew. You can never possess another person. It's wrong, Anthony, wrong. Don't do it."

"I'm *not*," I said. "I only thought she'd like to lie down."

"He's moving about too much," said Gillian. "Please stop him, Roger. Don't let him go sideways like that again."

"Is it right to tease your woman like that, Anthony? Is it right? Is it kind? I'm only asking you."

"I'm standing perfectly still. I shall go to bed," I said, with dignity, feeling suddenly hideously ill-used.

After a long, baffled moment, during which the door seemed to recede beyond any hope of ever getting to bed, I decided not to go after all, but to sit down where I was instead and concentrate on two matters which I found worrying—what sort of six o'clock was it, and where?

Roger was standing over me with a threatening look. There was a faint, dreadful dew upon his forehead.

"I might be sick," he said, challengingly.

Before I could deal with this situation, a new, a totally different voice, a voice with a crisp quality in it that struck me as being quite different from any voice I had been hearing recently, broke in upon us. It said:

"May I ask what you three think you are doing?"

It was Hester—Hester in a sensible dressing-gown, her beautiful hair in a pigtail, her blue eyes flashing.

"We must be at home," I said to Roger.

He did not answer. He was showing definite signs of being about to fulfil his threat. I looked hopefully at Gillian. Her eyes were tightly sealed in a face illuminated by a faint, greenish tinge. Her lips moved in a nervous manner.

"I don't think they feel well," I said feebly to Hester.

"Small wonder," said Hester. "*Small* wonder," she repeated.

Between each word her mouth like a hen's behind snapped smartly together.

"Such a *sight*." There was an implication here, I felt,

71

about the effect on an innocent, unborn child. "You ought all to be ashamed of yourselves."

"We are," I said, simply. It seemed, under the circumstances the best, the only, thing to say.

* * * * *

Years later my mother sat on the end of my bed and said:

"Really, Anto, darling, it was very naughty of you to encourage Roger."

"What's the time?" I asked feebly, keeping my eyes very stiff.

"Six o'clock."

"Oh, *no*—not six o'clock *again*?"

"Six p.m. that is—it was six a.m. when you upset Hester so."

"Did I upset her?"

"She said none of you knew where you were."

"I don't see why *she* should be upset by that—the thing is, she only came down in order to be upset—never a thought for us, all feeling so ill."

"The funny thing was," said my mother with genuine interest, "you'd put the car away terribly neatly."

"I don't remember a thing about it," I said fretfully. "You know what that awful old man's parties are like— I'm sure he's won big money from us all."

"Oh dear, were you playing poker?"

"I think so—I'm afraid so." My mind struggled rustily to remember and suddenly a terrible thought struck me. "Heavens, Mama, what day is it?"

"Wednesday, darling." She was poking idly at a loose strip of wallpaper near the head of my bed. "I really must get this room done up. Would you like a stripy, Regency paper? Only I'm never quite sure if they really had as much striped wallpaper as people seem to imagine. Do you think very dark olive green with a white ceiling—wouldn't that mirror look lovely against olive green?"

"Oh, lord, I'd forgotten all about it—I never told you and I've never met him."

My mother looked at me severely.

"Do try and be coherent, Anthony. I *will* say this for your father—he could hold his drink—none of you boys seem able to at all."

My mother had all her life supplied my father with unswerving devotion and constructive criticism—she loved to remember his great qualities aloud and, lest this should become boring to her listeners, she prefaced them always darkly, with "I *will* say this . . ." hinting at endless other things that could not and would not be said. But now I was not amused.

"Richmond was coming to-day; I had a wire from him just as we were moving off on Monday, and I'd forgotten all about it."

"I suppose then, it must be him that's just arrived."

"Just arrived? For God's sake! Where?"

"He's downstairs now, with Jane Harrington. She says he was wandering about the Shelbourne looking like an actor-manager, so she took him racing at Leopardstown and then brought him down here. *What* a good-looking man, dear, he reminds me very slightly of your uncle Rupert—in his good days of course, before he went so queer."

"Richmond never had any good days," I said sourly. "And this will be one of his very queerest, you'll see."

"But dear, he's being *so* charming."

"I'm sure he is." I shuddered slightly at the thought of

73

that studied and relentless charm. "You know I'm supposed to be finishing a play for him and not getting drunk at poker parties and hunting and racing? We must concoct a story."

"Can't you say you're getting local colour? I'm sure that's what people always do."

"Unfortunately, this play isn't even remotely connected with hunting or racing or playing poker."

"Then you can say you were giving your subconscious mind a chance to work on it," said my mother triumphantly. "I read about that in a book by a *very* knowledgeable man—a Penguin——"

"You're a divine woman—perhaps if *you* say it he'll believe it; you look so innocent. I must go and warn Gillian."

My mother frowned.

"Darling, you know I *never* interfere—are you going to marry Gillian some time soon, do you think?"

"It's what we came over here to do, really. You like her, don't you?"

"Oh, yes, I do, very much—I'd love to have you married, too—but don't you think that you and she are a little too alike to be altogether happy?"

"Darling—what would you choose for me—a fresh, solid country lass?"

My mother looked doubtful.

"Well, no, not *fresh* exactly—or *solid*—but perhaps somebody a little more stable than Gillian—not that I don't think she's sweet, mind you, and I daresay that horrid husband of hers upset her nerves. "

Jimmy Lodwick had been big and blond and full of good cheer, with an attractive body and an unattractive mind. A *faux bonhomme* if ever I saw one. His calculated generosity—he was very rich—had long been a source of despair and fascination to his friends, who were always hoping that *this* time there was no trap—but there always was. "If Jimmy ever casts his bread upon the waters," someone said once, "it's only because he knows damn well he's going to get it back with butter on."

"And what I hate," Gillian used to complain, "is that Jimmy never will give me a present—not even a *birthday* present—unless he's absolutely certain it's a good investment. God knows, darling, I'm as keen a girl as any on diamonds and gold shares and knick-knacks of Fabergé —but God knows also there are moments when I pine for cosier things—like that divine guinea-pig that he won't let me have—Mark my words, if I leave him it'll be because of that guinea-pig although everyone will say it's because of Rose Hillchester."

Which everyone did, of course. Gillian nowadays often got very worried about Andrew, in case he should resemble his father mentally, as he certainly did physically.

"I must teach Andrew to be sure and give people what they want and not what he thinks they ought to have— even if it's going to come to pieces in their hands the very next day."

"I'm sure Jane will teach him that," I had said, maliciously.

Now I kissed my mother and apologised for encouraging Roger, and went along to see Gillian. The curtains were drawn in her room, but the bedside lamp was on— she lay in a cosy huddle with half her face buried in the pillow, her mouth askew and her hair falling forward over her forehead. I could see one eye, smudgy with mascara but peacefully closed, a curve of cheek and some lipstick. She looked very innocent and unattractive and I felt a sudden rush of warm affection for her. It seemed a pity to wake her up but the eye opened directly I sat down on the bed.

"I wasn't asleep—what's the time?"

"Six o'clock."

"Oh, *no*."

She heaved round, shook her hair back and opened the other eye.

"Is it *always* six o'clock in this house?"

"If it is, it's very suitable for a land where it's always afternoon. Listen, my dear one, I've got a gorgeous piece of news for you."

"What is it?" She caught my eye. "Oh, *no*, Anthony, you're not to tell me. Is your mother going to throw us out?"

"Good heavens no. She said she couldn't think how we put the car away so neatly."

"Well, neither can I. Did we?"

"So it seems."

"Was Roger sick *in* the drawing-room?"

"I don't know. I haven't dared to ask. But listen to what I have to tell you. Richmond's here."

"Richmond?" She thought faintly for a moment. "Oh, goodness, you mean you never met him?"

"Exactly."

"How did he get here?"

"Jane picked him up in the Shelbourne and brought him down. They're both downstairs now."

"Oh, dear," said Gillian, "the *temperament* we'll have tomorrow."

76

"Tonight."

"I shan't come down tonight. I'm indisposed."

"You'll certainly come down tonight. You're my woman, aren't you?"

"Roger kept saying that, didn't he? Last night—I mean this morning. Oh dear, how terribly badly behaved we've all been. I daren't face Nanny and she's got all my clothes—she keeps getting away with them all—I might as well be in Holloway."

At that very moment Nanny came bustling in, small and fierce, and hung some clothes in the wardrobe and began to bustle out again, wordlessly. Her face expressed that it was not for her to question the ways of the gentry. Gillian eyed her fearfully over the sheets. I caught her apron and pulled her back as she was going out of the door.

"Listen, Nanny, take that horrid look off your face. We're very ill."

"That's my clean apron, Anthony, if you don't mind."

"Don't be fierce, Nanny. I'm not feeling strong enough."

Nanny's face softened.

"I will say you do look poorly, you and Mrs. Lodwick, both, poor things. I've told you again and again, you're not one who can miss your sleep."

"No, Nanny, you're so right. And as I have missed it, and so has Mrs. Lodwick and we both feel so poorly on account of it, will you be a perfect love and bring us a tiny drink up here, just to set us up?"

"You don't deserve it, either of you. I say that straight out."

Nanny disappeared.

"Will she bring it?" asked Gillian.

"Of course."

"How fascinating. I'd always heard of twistings round little fingers, but I've never actually seen it happen before."

She hadn't, as it turned out, seen it happen then. Nanny, indeed, was soon back, and bearing glasses on a tray, but she wore an air of quiet triumph and the glasses were brimming over with delicious, fresh, unutterably revolting milk.

"I'll just wait here while you drink it, and then take the glasses down, it will save a trip."

She stood at the foot of the bed with a Tibetan lack of expression and watched us drink. No naughty children had ever yet got the better of Nanny—no naughty children could ever before have had so cruel a punishment.

Richmond had arranged himself in front of the Adam mantelpiece and was giving Jane his famous sulky Grecian profile and the fullest view of his beautiful, strong and nervous right hand holding strongly and beautifully a glass of sherry. This necessitated his talking to Aunt Emmy, who was completely hypnotised and had let her cigar go out. Hester was almost equally impressed, perched on the end of the sofa in a flowing, flowered robe of non-committal cut. My mother was knitting a sock in a gentle and dignified manner. Roger was happily engaged with the whisky in a corner while letting Hubert's explanation of the patent adjustable clinch-pins on the power take-off of the new Allis-Beaker tractor flow over his head. Andrew was ranging around Jane like a nervous planet, plying her with drink and cigarettes in an effort to take her mind off Richmond.

Jane, conscious of a really exquisite effort by Creed, was enjoying herself a lot.

The impression that I got as I followed Gillian in was that Richmond had become a regular race-goer but all conversation ceased abruptly and several pairs of accusing eyes were turned on us. Richmond's smile became steely with charm.

"*Here* you are, darlings, at last."

He waved aside my admittedly useless apologies.

"Don't think that I blame you in the *very* least, Anthony. How could anyone leave all this——" he waved his sherry slightly and patronisingly at Aunt Emmy—"Everybody has always told me about the great, great charm of Ireland, and they were absolutely right."

Roger rose, and came to Gillian with a leer.

"What are you going to drink, dear?"

"What would mix with milk?" asked Gillian faintly.

Richmond raised one eyebrow in his celebrated, quizzical manner. His expression implied that this was overplaying it a bit, even for quaint charm.

"Milk, Gillian?" he enquired crisply.

"Nanny brought me up some milk just now," said Gillian coldly.

"But how breathlessly *right*. Nanny. Of course." Richmond bared his teeth slightly at her and turned back to Aunt Emmy.

"I'm very ignorant about racing and there's something I want very much to know—I'm sure *you* will be able to tell me. . . . It's dreadful to feel so ignorant . . ."

"Damn, damn, damn," whispered Gillian, receiving her drink from Roger. "What terrible friends you have, Anthony. I simply *can't* bear to have him here—spoiling everything—sneering at Nanny and Aunt Emmy . . ."

"Don't be so sensitive, darling. You know perfectly well they're going to enjoy every minute of it madly—when have you ever known Aunt Emmy let her cigar go out before?"

"It's true for Anthony," said Roger. "Nanny has already taken his pyjamas away to air them, and I think she's planning Ovaltine in bed for him—she says he's too thin for his height—he'll be sorry he ever thought milk was funny."

Hubert, who had been wading helplessly in the depths of our conversation, clutched desperately at this factual straw.

"All very well to say milk's *funny*—but if people *knew* something about the difficulties of producing it—*clean* milk, that is to say . . ."

He gave Richmond a beady glance and began edging a way towards him.

"Oh, what heaven," said Gillian. "He's going to tell him about the all-electric Allis-Beaker milking machine with patented adjustable hip-hinges."

"It will be an egotistical free-for-all then," I said. "Richmond will tell him about Peter Brook's production of *Huis Clos*—I wonder which will be the most bored?"

But Richmond was listening very attentively to Aunt Emmy explaining everything that he had always wanted to know about steeplechasing; while he remained happily conscious of Jane's calm speculative glance and Andrew's restive misery. Hubert was only able to get as far as Hester and, having got there, he asked her how she felt tonight, eh? Hester, who had momentarily quite forgotten that she ought to be feeling anything, brightened visibly and said that perhaps she would go to bed not *too* late just tonight. Her gallantry affected Hubert, who sat down on the arm of the sofa and massaged her shoulder lovingly.

"I'm sure that's *just* the way he oils clinch-pins," murmured Gillian into her drink.

"Don't be m-malicious," said Roger.

He was getting slightly slurred, and he put down his glass and reached for the decanter with just too much deliberation. It was when I saw, then, the tenderness and anxiety of Gillian's sideways glance that I wondered for an instant—but had no time to wonder as Thomas Quin suddenly announced from the doorway, in a jerky mutter:

"Mr. Molloy's come now," and Conor advanced, smilingly, in muddy boots and breeches and a slightly torn coat and with just a trace of dried blood across the bridge of his nose and one cheek—so perfect a picture of a tough young man pleasantly relaxed after heroic and exhausting outdoor sport that I could almost feel Richmond stiffening angrily.

Conor was explaining himself to my mother in his thick, sing-song, twangy Tipperary voice that Oxford had, happily, failed to influence. "I hadn't the trailer out and they ran right away from me and the mare's half-dead—I wondered could she have a sup here before I'd go on?"

"Of course, Conor—have you put her in a box? Roger, tell Micky——"

But Roger had put down his drink and was already going. He would probably see to the mare himself—rub dry her ears and throat and back, muffle her in rugs with straw beneath them, give her a bottle of stout to drink and then prepare a feed, hard or soft, large or small, according to her degree of exhaustion. He would talk softly to her in his slurred voice and breathe whisky at her as he pulled her ears and she would nudge at his shoulder with her nose and nibble at the back of his neck as he bent to rub her chest and delight in this unaccustomed gentleness.

"Had you a good day?" my mother was asking Conor.

"We'd a great run from Killanure, very fast indeed, but we marked him below at Murphy's—'twas a great pity, for the bitches are in need of blood——"

Richmond's eyebrow was rising steadily. I think he slightly suspected that I had somehow cast and produced Conor in this enthralling part.

"And who was out?" asked Aunt Emmy.

We were all gathering round Conor like well-trained hawks to a lure. The hold that fox hunting has over its disciples it as frightening as it is fascinating. Conor would tell us that Paddy Casey had been trying to sell his grey horse and the lad had given it a crucifying fall over wire; that the puppy Aunt Emmy had walked was still inclined to babble; that they had gone away very fast from Killanure and several people had been left; that Mike Harrington's English horse had flown a stone-faced bank—"the sight went from my eyes to see the lep he made"; that hounds had split on a fresh fox, but Tommy had managed to stop them; that Euphemia Coke had jumped a "hell of a big, dirty drain like Becher's Brook" on her four-year-old by Tartan; and on these words we would hang, wide-eyed, like children learning about Father Christmas. I had often tried to analyse this fearful fascination; to work out for myself exactly what the black magic consists of, and I had come to the conclusion that it must be because fox hunting provides, mentally and physically, the perfect form of escapism, the perfect reaction from the dreary twentieth-century myth of Progress and the perfectibility of man. To begin with, even before one has got on one's horse, there is the dressing-up in traditional clothes—and anybody who does not enjoy dressing up is fit only for treasons, stratagems and spoils—and not really even for those since he will not enjoy being in disguise. Then, I do not believe that M. Sartre himself could deny the romance implicit in the sight and sound of galloping horses, and the power and glory of being a part of this speed and strength and, if one is lucky, in control of it—this rare sensation might have even seduced Oscar Wilde if he had once tried it—might indeed, yet, seduce a Sitwell. Add to this that ancient, incalculable, irresistible lure, the spice of authentic danger, and you have the perfect, the complete, sweet, oblivious antidote, which will for the space of forty-five minutes from Kilquin Gorse raze out the written troubles of the brain as if they had been written on a slate and a damp sponge had been passed across them.

"In this the patient must minister to himself," and a psychiatrist prescribing three days' hunting a week would, I am sure, have the very greatest success. For no one— not if he has drunk too much the night before; not if he has lain awake with a mind reeling restively amongst the metaphysics of Donne, the philosophy of Seneca, and the psychology of Jung—only to find at 2 a.m. that Soneryl has the laugh on them all; not if he has woken groaning, suspecting cancer of the liver and hating the sight of his boots; not even he will fail to be healed by the splendid immediacy of the moment when the little black horse (grabbing cunningly at his bit in the hope of getting his head free enough to buck on the far side) faces the stone-faced bank which Mike Harrington's horse has just flown with such superb disregard of the law of gravity—whilst behind, advancing in a crescendo of bounds and snorting like a steam engine, Euphemia Coke's four-year-old is showing unmistakable signs that if you and the little black horse do not jump both quickly and cleanly there is every possibility that you and the little black horse will yourselves be jumped upon, heavily and hideously, by Euphemia Coke and her four-year-old.

So Conor held us spellbound with his commonplace tale until they had again marked him below at Murphy's and the bitches had sung hopelessly above his cosy ramifications in the big double bank—"sure, that one would never do a hand's turn stopping, only if you'd give him gold for it, and not then unless you'd stand over him"—and then Conor, smiling serenely, rivalling Richmond in charm, even if of a rougher kind, had said:

" 'Twas a great party we had last night—but sure, your garage door is too narrow—I thought I'd never get the car in without knocking it."

"Oh, it was *you*," said my mother. "But how did you get home, Conor?"

"I walked. A couple of miles across the fields, you know, is all it is."

It was too much.

"How very kind of you", said Gillian, coldly, "to take such care of us. You must be very tired."

"Not a bit of it," said Conor cheerfully.

Certainly he didn't look tired. He looked healthy and

handsome and, I considered, rather insolent, and far from being a fit mate for Caroline. A cold and atavistic antagonism stirred deeply in my bowels and shivered the roots of my hair as I met his triumphant eye. Then I was aware that Jane was looking at me; and what Jane looked at—and put two and two together about—and then embellished with her own style of extravagant and malicious mockery, would start the subtle tom-toms of the bush telegraph throbbing around the dinner-tables of Limerick, amongst the Dublin hotel bars and through the mountains to the furthest summer palaces of Kerry. Hastily and unnecessarily I provided Aunt Emmy with an ash-tray. But Jane had missed nothing.

"Darling Anthony," she said to me happily as she left. "And I always thought you were such a civilised one."

Chapter Six

Roger was packing the case to go in the back of the little green car.

"How delicious," said Gillian, looking into it nervously. "Do we quite honestly need as much whisky as that?" Roger rightly ignored her and went on packing. "Oh dear," said Gillian. She sat down at the littered breakfast table and peered unenthusiastically at the bacon and eggs that Thomas Quin set unsteadily before her. Gillian always suffered from squirrels in the stomach before hunting. "I don't care for meets at Garnagarry," she announced now, putting a fork into her egg as though she expected it to jump at her.

"Why not?" asked Hubert, chewing steadily away like Mr. Gladstone. "It's our best meet."

"I know. That's the *very* reason I don't like it, Hubert, darling."

"I don't know what you mean," said Hubert, taking a long pull at his coffee and letting his mind drift back to the goggle valves on the super-extendable depth-adjustable root drill that he had seen advertised in the *Farmer and Stockbreeder*.

"*Because* it's our best meet people come from the Limerick and ride jealous. After a field or so I get inspired to ride jealous myself and knock them off the tops of banks. *Heavens*, how I frightened myself last time!"

"Then why do it?" asked Hubert sensibly.

"You know how it is—one just can't resist."

"I can, easily." He got up to get himself some more bacon.

"Of course you can, sweet. It's well known that the devil is in absolute despair over you."

Hubert came slowly back to the table, frowning slightly, chewing on the cud of this idea in the hope that it might yield something digestible in time. It didn't; but as he had long ago decided that Gillian was not only childish but Rather Odd, his face soon cleared into its usual happy and ingenuous absorption in solid and preferably mechanical fact, and he opened *The Times* portentously.

"Oh, dear," said Gillian restively. "You haven't even looked, Hubert, to see if anybody's born. Do just slip me the outside, there's a sweet."

"Of course somebody's born," said Hubert placidly. "People are born every day." He went on reading without slipping her the outside.

"Don't interrupt your father while he's reading *The Times*," I said. "Eat up like a good girl, or Nanny will give you hell."

"I don't seem to feel very hungry. I'll just have some more coffee."

"Gillian," said Aunt Emmy suddenly, looking up from Volume XXXI of the Stud Book, which she had open beside her plate, "I'm giving you the little black horse today."

"The little black horse, Aunt Emmy?"

"He's great over those big doubles around Garnagarry. I'm sure you'll enjoy him."

She beamed at Gillian, taking a simple pleasure in the thought of her coming delight.

"Oh, Aunt Emmy, it *is* sweet of you," said Gillian faintly. "But wouldn't you rather have him yourself?"

"Roger and I must take the babies out."

"I'm sure the little black horse is heaven, Aunt Emmy—but won't he buck me off almost immediately?"

"Ah, he might give the least bit of a hoist before he'll settle. Sure, it's only his play," said Aunt Emmy, defensively.

Gillian looked hopelessly round the table at us.

"You may laugh, you brutes," she said savagely, "but Micky told me only yesterday the little black horse would shake a mustard plaster loose if his mind was on it."

"But his mind won't be on it," said Roger, comfortingly. "His mind will be on getting to hounds, you'll see."

"Really, you needn't worry, Gillian," said my mother helpfully. "Micky loves to pretend that all the horses are very dangerous and barely rideable even by him. All grooms do."

"And they're generally dead right." Gillian refused to be comforted or helped. "Anthony, I should like, if you've quite finished laughing, a little dash of brandy in my coffee."

"I tell you what," said Andrew helpfully, "you could swop with me."

"And have that chestnut horse of Mike's that thinks it's still running in the Grand Military? Never, never let it be said that I'm lacking in mother love, and I quite freely admit I've lain awake all night thinking about you on it— all the sa... ...r you than me."

"It's Jane wh... ...horse," said Andrew, looking casually ...

"Oh, you unna... ...lian stirred the brandy into her coffee ... brightened slightly. "I wonder if it ... ...y confidential brown animal?"

"You mean you... ...nly son?" I asked.

"Abraham woul... ...," said Gillian calmly.

Hubert rustled *The Times* and coughed slightly.

"I'm sure nobody need sacrifice anybody," said my mother cosily. "Emmy, weren't you giving Anthony the grey? Couldn't he and Gillian change?"

Gillian gave me an indescribable glance of leering triumph.

"Now listen to me," I said. "I am a soft semi-intellectual, my endurance weakened by long attendance at first nights. If I hunt, it's going to be for my health and I don't consider the little black horse healthy."

"Gillian's going to sacrifice her son and Anthony's going to sacrifice his future wife," said Roger delightedly. "What we need is more of a Round Table spirit."

"Oh, look," said Gillian, "there they go, the horrible sweets."

There they went, past the window, swinging shoulders, flirting heads, plaited manes, creaking of saddlery and ring of bits. First went one of Matty's underlings, a boy called Micky, half-witted and highly religious (Roger always declared that he was bound to end up a saint) perched on the grey horse and leading the little black horse, and the roan mare for Hubert. A decent distance behind came Matty sitting very tight on one baby and holding the other one very tight also, so that its muzzle appeared to be clamped to his knee. They had been clipped and had attained a certain air of sophistication in consequence, but their wildly roving eyes and semaphoring ears belied this. They were bonny babies and obviously prepared to bounce at the very slightest excuse. This was offered to them immediately by Thomas Quin, who suddenly shook a duster out of the drawing-room window— whether innocently or not would have been hard to say. There was always apt to be cold war between Thomas Quin and the stables.

The babies were electrified at such unnatural phenomena. The led one immediately bolted for two feet or so and then, finding that Matty had retained the end of the reins and it could go no further, yielded to circumstances and swung in a wild half-circle like a ship at anchor, around the head of its horrified comrade, ending up on the far side with its bit pulled half through its mouth and Matty's arm clamped irretrievably across his chest. The baby he rode had at the same time jumped forward and sideways, and ahead the little black horse, annoyed at the unseemly scuffling behind him, suddenly humped himself and lashed out warningly.

"Oh, *dear*," said Gillian faintly.

"They're grand and gay in themselves," said Aunt Emmy, pleasedly.

"Oh, Aunt Emmy, honey—how can you be so heartless?"

Matty, by some miracle of contortion, had managed to hold on to both babies and to turn his mount round. They ended up facing each other, with popping eyes, uttering the long, hysterical, rolling snorts which they thought the occasion deserved.

With cajoling and chirruping and soft calling upon the saints Matty straightened them out and rode doggedly on, casting a glance of bitter contempt at the drawing-room window.

"Won't they be late, Emmy?" asked my mother.

"Oh, no, they're going by the bog road—it's not three miles."

The bog road would run, grey and rutted, across the brown and gold and blue of the bog, all merging into mist under the soft morning rain. The air would smell of peat-turf, the brown cliffs left where the turf had been cut in the summer would look like slabs of rich chocolate cake and the brown peat water would be thick with rushes in the ditches. Curlews would call, smoky self-sufficient donkeys would gaze contemptuously at the invaders of their lonely kingdom and goats, hobbled two by two and each pulling a different way, would lurch frantically out of the horses' path.

"I must show you the bog one day," I said to Gillian. "You might think it hideous or beautiful, but it's quite unique."

"I think I saw some, coming down from Dublin."

"Only a small, dull piece. Ours is much nicer."

"Anthony used to love it," said Roger. "He'd sit there for hours, dreaming about theatres."

"And now I sit in theatres for hours dreaming about the bog."

"It's too sad," said Gillian. "Just like Bernard Shaw said."

"What did he say?"

"He said there's only one thing worse than not getting your heart's desire, and that's getting it. I think it was him," she added doubtfully.

"There's a lot of good land going to waste in the bogs," said Hubert. "If they got a proper drainage scheme going they could reclaim a lot of it. It's amazing what my little grab, even, has done in the boggy meadows."

He got up and brushed toast crumbs from his waistcoat and went upstairs to see Hester, who had taken to breakfast in bed as a protest against strong men lying in bed in the mornings.

"Hubert is really wonderful," said my mother loyally. "It's all very well for you to laugh, Anthony, but where would we be without him? Tell me that."

"It's jealousy that makes him laugh," said Roger. "And me too. Sorry, Mama." He went round the table and kissed the top of her head. He was apologising for his own comparative lack of sterling usefulness. My mother patted him vaguely. Roger was a warming and lightening companion and Hubert was a male Martha—in her all-embracing charity there was room for them both.

All this time Richmond had been very quietly and unobtrusively nourishing himself with grapefruit ("nasty, unripe things," Nanny had said, "No wonder he's thin") black coffee and an Egyptian cigarette. He had obviously decided, before dressing, on the part he was to play. He would be self-effacing, but at the same time subtly mysterious. Never let it be said that he didn't know what clothes to wear in the country—yet still one could be in the country but not of it. He had borrowed an old hacking jacket of Roger's and he wore his own corduroy trousers (I could not believe that the props man had not just spent half an hour making them dirty) and a pair of broken-down flying boots. It was all entirely suitable and bogus. He sat smoking, withdrawn, gazing with noble sadness into the gentle rain outside. Impossible not to be moved by that grave and flawless beauty—almost equally impossible to realise that it was the outward and visible sign of an entire lack of spiritual grace.

"Mr. Kerr," said my mother, "I wonder if it would bore you very much to follow with me in the car?"

Richmond inclined himself towards her with gentle courtesy.

"I have always longed to hunt and never had the time or opportunity," he said. "Far from being bored, I can't tell you how excited I am." He caressed an eager Labrador head, and gave it a bit of bacon rind off Hubert's plate with the quiet distinction of a true artist who likes dogs and horses.

*   *   *   *   *

Garnagarry might be referred to as a village, except that a village implies a certain extent of cosiness, and in this Garnagarry, like all places of its type in Ireland, was singularly lacking being, indeed, hideous and dreary in the extreme. It could not really be referred to as a town either, although its main street was impressively and excessively wide, however devastatingly it might crumble at the edges, however blocked it might be with donkey-carts and conversational men with bicycles. (No bicycle-owner in Ireland ever addresses a word to another bicycle-owner, except in the middle of a main street.)

Garnagarry was an unreasonable out-crop of human

habitations sprawled bleakly around a cross-roads and here you might have a drink perhaps, on your way down to Mallow, in Mick O'Connor's dark bar and learn who would be trying in the Novice 'Chase (carefully avoiding the more elegant façade of Delany's Hotel, flat-fronted on to the main street, with its lounge where only local boys went, wishing to impress their girls; full of oilcloth and bamboo, glass-topped tables, everlasting flowers and advertisements of last year's hunt balls and elderly serial films).

Here were the usual mouldering rows of little stucco-fronted houses, some grey, some white-washed, one or two painted pink or green in an attempt at gaiety that had soon been allowed to lapse again into dirt and crumbling plaster; here was the draughty garage where slow boys masquerading as mechanics in oily overalls quickly ruined any of the swift American cars that might be unwise enough to stop here during their tearing journeys down the long road from Dublin to Cork; here was the Guard Barracks where law kept happy company with disorder; here were the little shops, each selling everything and each—as advertised in the *Tipperary Star* or the *Nationalist* —the finest business in the South; here at the cross-roads, was the pump from which the entire population drew their supply of water (luckily nobody washed very much and Guinness was more popular as a drink); here, set back a little way down the narrow, dusty minor road, was the Big House—fading into the landscape behind its impressive wrought-iron gates, one of its square, crumbling rooms occupied by a cheerfully unsuccessful farmer who rented grazing to Pat Delaney—Pat Delaney's brood mares, hidden beneath layers of mud and scurf and stumbling over their neglected feet, would very likely produce a future Grand National winner.

Poverty broods like a miasma over Irish provincial towns. Their air of having been roughly run up for no particular reason and being about to crumble away again affronts the eye accustomed to rose-smothered Porlock cottages, Cotswold villages grown from their native stone, and the wealthy enormities of the Thames Valley— affronts it; causes it to withdraw; and draws it again irresistibly, to their secret and deadly charm.

So now, I was delighted to see Garnagarry again, to set foot in the grey and rainy street and to be going to have a drink at Mick O'Connor's. The bar where the Irishman assembles to drink his Guinness and his Jameson and Paddy resembles its English counterpart even less than does the place in which it stands. The inn as the English know it is totally absent—there is still no trace of cosiness: no pewter, fires, dart-boards, cleanliness, rambler roses, fat spaniels, or painted signs—the Irish bar (there were eight in the main street of Garnagarry) is very often situated in one dark and dirty corner of a general shop, where pigs'-heads, tin baths and rubber boots hang about in the gloom in indiscriminate clusters and smelly old women in unhygienic black shawls buy barmbrack at one counter, while happy foxhunters take their jumping-powder at another and a small and filthy-faced child sits cosily by the not very warming stove and is given a taste of this and that. Such was Mick O'Connor's bar and this morning it was loud with activity, blue with cigarette smoke and full of the ring of coins and what are you drinking? The West Tipperary Foxhounds were milling in mournful excitement in the yard behind Delaney's

Hotel, and the wide main street was full of horse-boxes and trailers and their anxious, whinnying occupants—one of whom was, at the moment we approached, successfully blocking the entrance to Mick O'Connor's. A large, ugly and irritable horse, he was sidling slowly backwards along the pavement, endeavouring to rub his rider off.

"He has my knee broke," this youth cheerfully informed us. "Mind now", he called to Richmond who was incautiously approaching, "that he wouldn't let a crack at you, not meaning any harm."

The horse lifted a hind leg tentatively.

"My God," said Richmond, forgetting his restrained role, and leapt agilely backwards into the road. Here he was smartly buffeted by the quarters of a revolving grey pony who was having hysterics because its stable companion had been led two yards away from it.

"You can't imagine", Gillian said cheerfully to him, "how *divinely* silly horses always are."

Richmond carefully took up a moderately safe position with his back against the shop window and facing the divinely silly horse who didn't mean any harm.

"Get on now, do, Seumas," said Aunt Emmy to his rider. "Can't you see you're blocking the doorway for us?"

"God help us, miss, would you ever lead him on a bit and I'd likely get started?"

Aunt Emmy led him away down the road lecturing him as she went and we pushed our way into the smoke and uproar of the bar.

"Have you ever drunk port and brandy together?" Roger asked Richmond, who replied cautiously that it sounded very interesting. "It keeps the wind out," said

Roger, "and it'll get you over the first bank when the stones look cold to you in the morning," and he began to burrow his way through the crowd.

"Whatever does he mean?" Richmond asked Gillian.

"Well, they just *do* look cold you know—cold and perfectly hideous."

Richmond offered her a cigarette rather hopelessly and looked around him at the unlikely scene. In this drab setting Freddy and Poodle and old Dicky shone in all their rich glory, and their Ritz bar voices, high and elegant, sang the latest scandal of the race courses over their dollops of port-and-brandy; enlivened by interjections in the vernacular from quiet little men in loud tweeds, excitable priests in suitable black breeches, local girls making good in wide-brimmed bowlers and johdpurs, and burly, knowing figures who had the next Gold Cup winner stabled in Delaney's yard. Here too, Colonel Wilbraham, bursting unselfconsciously out of his old, stained pink, happily stood drinks to the fierce, smart Limerick thrusters while listening with half an ear to the cunning babble of Paddy Casey, who stood at his elbow trying to sell him a horse. "Only a big man like yourself, Colonel, would appreciate the way it wouldn't take a feather out of him to carry you." Here the Lady Euphemia, lurking in a very dark corner beneath the pigs'-heads, talked very long and earnestly to a nondescript little man with an innocent face.

"Look at Little Daisy fixing J. J.," said Roger. "If only I could hear the divils, I might make a fortune."

"That's J. J. Connors," I told Richmond, "the famous —or infamous, whichever way you see it—steeplechase jockey."

"Sure, he's a great jock," said somebody, perceiving Richmond to be a stranger and showing off with happy pride. "That one could lose by a nostril and you'd never know did he mean it."

"How extraordinary," said Richmond and looked as if he meant it.

For what, I think, may have been the first time in his life, he was completely baffled by his surroundings.

"Now tell me, absolutely honestly," the gorgeous Poodle was saying to Mick O'Connor, sweating in his shirt-sleeves behind the bar, "will your mare give his Lordship a good ride round on Thursday?"

"Most times he would, now," said Mick O'Connor, leaning heavily on an elbow to consider the matter and frowning thoughtfully. "And more times he wouldn't," he finally pronounced cautiously.

"Oh, God, darling, did you hear?" enquired Poodle of the room at random.

Her sad query was lost in the general brouhaha as a rumour suddenly started that hounds had moved off and that old George had said he was sick to death of blowing bloody dipsomaniacs out of bloody bars and was just going to sneak quietly away. It was well known that old George disliked meeting at Garnagarry as much as Gillian did, and for much the same reason, and that he might easily fulfil his threat. So we all emerged reluctantly into the rainy street and grooms began to sweep rugs off shuddering horses, while their employers tinkered nervously with their spur straps to avoid the inevitable moment of stripping camel hair and leopard skin and being heartlessly "put up".

Micky came grinning towards us with his three charges.

The little black horse slithered slightly in the gutter, laid back his ears, and squealed.

"Up you get, Andrew darling," said Gillian firmly.

Andrew was in a dilemma. Mike and Jane had not yet arrived. They sometimes indulged in what Aunt Emmy considered the shockingly decadent habit of sending their horses straight to the first draw. If Andrew was to ride Jane's horse it would mean also a ride in Jane's car and Mike would be driving. On the other hand, it would be rather magnificent to lean casually down from the squealing black and explain to Jane how nervous it made his mother. He pondered and Gillian watched him ponder and grinned lovingly to herself.

"Look," said Roger to me, "there's the horse Paddy was trying to sell old Wilbraham. It's a divil to pull. Watch me tease the lad."

He went up to a small, calm boy perched on an enormous, excited horse.

"Pulling you, is he, Tommy?" he enquired sympathetically.

"Pull is it?" The scorn and pity were most magnificently mingled. "God help you——"

Here the effect was very slightly spoilt as the horse, perceiving inattention, made a sudden, grinding grab at its twisted snaffle and ducked its head down to its fetlocks, dragging the boy half-way down its steely neck. But he came up undismayed, gasping virtuously:

"This one wouldn't pull the skin off a rice-pudding."

Roger wandered back to us, grinning, and Matty put him up on the more horrified of the two babies. It was actually the chestnut filly which Gillian and I had caught in the front avenue at Knockmoree the day I arrived.

"I told you she'd be handy by March," said Aunt Emmy happily to me.

"My dearest Aunt, I shan't be here in March and if I was nothing would induce me to ride anything in any race."

"Ah well, you'd never know."

"I *do* know."

Aunt Emmy ignored me and levered herself heavily on to the remaining baby, who almost immediately became middle-aged and nonchalant beneath her quiet hands. She and Roger walked their mounts off down the road, so that they would be at the back and out of the crowd when hounds moved off.

"Aren't they wonderful," said Gillian, looking after them. "If it was you or I darling, those terrible babies would be twined round somebody's car or gone through a shop window. Why doesn't Roger ride the filly in Aunt Emmy's horrible race?"

"I could take offence."

"But you won't, sweet."

"No. Roger can't ride races because (a) he's too heavy and (b) he'd get plastered before he weighed out."

"I do think it's very kind and forgiving of you, Anthony, to put it in that order."

Andrew was still haplessly debating with himself on the pavement, looking very large and beautiful in the combined cast-off clothing of Roger, Hubert and myself. It is a curious but undoubtedly established fact that clothes once cut by a master hand will continue to show their origin even on people whom they were never intended to fit. These touched Andrew too closely in some places and not at all in others, yet the magic of Peal and Tautz shone forth undimmed and lent him confidence in himself as a rival of the magnificent Mike.

"Come on, darling," said Gillian, poking him in the ribs. "Jane will adore you on this dashing black creature, sacrificing yourself for your frail old Mum."

Andrew tried to frown coldly at her, but being really rather a nice boy, was overcome by unwilling laughter. At that moment the big Cadillac came swooping in a masterly way through the clutter, with Mike idly spinning the wheel with one hand while he lit a cigarette and Jane leaning lusciously back looking into a gold flapjack and giving herself a fresh mouth. They looked exactly like an advertisement in the *New Yorker*.

"Heavens, how I adore those two," said Gillian. "They do cast such a gorgeous glow, don't they—if they run out of capital any wise government would subsidise them at once—but of course they won't."

But I had just seen something much more exciting— Caroline riding down the road towards us, looking velvety and gold and creamy and altogether pleasing on a gay, Araby little horse sidling pleasantly along on tip-toe. She waved at us and went past without stopping in a very masterly way. I thought happily that she had all the right instincts, even if she didn't know it. And then Conor Molloy came clattering out of the same side road from which Caroline had appeared, lounging at ease on a big, hot, head-shaking steeplechaser in the making. He shouted to us that he wouldn't stop, the horse wouldn't stand. I got up on the grey and bided my time.

Gillian and Andrew had gone over to talk to Jane and Mike and presently Andrew came back and got up on the black horse with an air of calm rectitude. Hounds had been let out of Delaney's yard and were flowing around old George, who sat angrily in the middle of the road, showering loving imprecations on them while Tommy Dwyer whipped Winifred away from something delicious she had found under a trailer and rated Reveller for taking an interest in a spitting kitten hiding on a window-ledge. Then off went old George and off went hounds and Tommy Dwyer and Poodle and Freddy and old Dicky and the Limerick visitors and the dealers and priests and jockeys and the children thrusting madly on self-reliant ponies. But I waited, fingering my perfectly tight girths, much to the grey horse's horror and indignation, until back down the road came Conor and Caroline, with the big horse out-walking the little one so fast that I was able to fall alongside her with the greatest ease.

As we passed the stationary Cadillac, waiting politely at the side of the road until every horse had gone by, Jane put her eyelashes out of the window at me and gave me a long, lascivious wink.

Chapter Seven

The rain drifted steadily and gently into our faces as we waited outside Kilgarvan; the soft, dilatory rain that seems to have no effect at all until, quite suddenly, you find you are soaked to the skin. It was warm, and already the more excitable amongst the horses were wreathed in clouds of steam.

"Rotten scenting day," observed Colonel Wilbraham, planted like an enormous happy blancmange on his weight-carrying roan and already started on his sandwiches.

"If only you didn't eat all the time, Willy, you wouldn't be so fat," observed his wife, plaintively and indisputably. She rode side-saddle in a correct and lady-like style, her reins held up delicately near her magnificent bosom, her scalloped hair twirled into a shining Chelsea bun; she swayed stiffly to the movements of her plain and amorous mare who had such a passion for her stable companion and followed him so closely and determinedly over every jump that disaster always seemed to be imminent between them.

"What is so wonderful", Roger had told me, "is, when the Colonel and his good lady quarrel and try to ride away from each other in injured dignity and the horses refuse to go."

"You've made it up?" Gillian had asked delightedly.

"I swear I haven't. Wait till you see. She once said to me, 'The good dumb creatures set us an example.'"

"You've made *that* up, Roger. I just don't believe you, that's all."

"Wait till you see."

The Colonel ate his sandwiches happily and talked in a bluff man-to-man way with old Heffernan, the owner of the covert, who was standing near him holding a thin greyhound which, half-crazy with rage and frustration, was making a good bid at strangling itself.

"There'd be a fox in there now," said old Heffernan. "Didn't I see him myself only yesterday, would be as big as a tiger; if they'd only get him out."

"Feller ought to build us a *machan*, what?" said the Colonel, delightedly slapping his thigh.

In Kilgarvan there was an almost dead silence, broken only from time to time by slightly peevish cries of encouragement from old George. Once a hound spoke dolefully and uncertainly and then decided against it. Kilgarvan was a large, straggling place, always badly stopped and very difficult to get a fox away from—but old Heffernan was a large cattle-dealer with a lot of land around Garnagarry and a fantastic quantity of money in roving cheques. So Kilgarvan remained the first draw from the best meet and Poodle and old Dicky gossiped in a far corner of the field with an odd Pytchley collar who had just flown over and smoked endless cigarettes and would have gone straight on to Speke by themselves only it would give old George apoplexy, but *really* darling, he *is* the quaintest old character, but such a sweet when he isn't being bloody, only he *will not* be teased and I must say I could rather admire him for it, couldn't you? Of this group were Jane and Mike, and Andrew was also in it, although not entirely of it, but all the same pretending that he was, hoping that Gillian and I wouldn't come up and spoil it and that, if we did, we wouldn't bring Aunt Emmy. For even the very nicest boy of eighteen may feel like this at times.

But poor Andrew was doomed to suffer hideously in quite a different way, for the little black horse had not, as Roger had promised, got his mind on getting to hounds, since hounds were obviously for the moment not gettable-to. His back was humped and he was waiting for an excuse to break loose. It was offered him when Mike's Grand Military lunatic suddenly jumped wildly sideways as a very tiny bird flew silently out of the hedge beside him.

The very next second Andrew was sitting on the muddy ground with his mouth slightly open and his bowler over one eye, while the little black horse careered round the field in a mad gaiety of misdirected energy.

"The young gentleman is gone," remarked old Heffernan placidly.

"Loose horse," bawled Colonel Wilbraham commandingly, although nobody could have failed to see it.

Unkindest cut of all, it was the shrill, excited trumpeting of Aunt Emmy's baby that lured the little black horse into stopping and sidling up and sniffing and finally being caught by Aunt Emmy, and it was Jane who cantered gaily across the field and could be seen to be laughing with Aunt Emmy before she brought him back to his crestfallen rider, who was unhappily having mud rubbed off his back by the delighted Poodle, who thought he was a sweet thing. Mike, a very generous man, told a comforting tale about how exactly the same thing had happened to him on a hell of a parade at Meerut and Andrew cheered up very slightly.

"Oh, the poor poppet," said Gillian. "The *good* it will do him, he'll be quite a pet now."

She was safely and happily ensconced on the very confidential brown animal and was looking almost prim. Every fly-button seemed to be secure and I had refused to allow her to wear a diamond brooch in her stock.

("But it's all I've got, darling?"

"I'll lend you a lovely plain gold bar from Woolworth's."

"You brute.")

Still no hopeful sounds came from Kilgarvan. A grinning hound, full of good-will, slipped out beside us, feathered in rather a hopeless way along the dry ditch, and went back again.

"That Reveller's a grand worker," said Colonel Wilbraham, showing off slightly.

It was not only not Reveller, but a bitch, and I kept silent, hoping for more.

Suddenly and for no apparent reason, there went round the field one of those groundless rumours that always occur at a large covert and we all galloped mildly and rather aimlessly across the field we were in and through a gap and down a cart-track and then stopped and galloped back again.

"I bet you don't know why you're doing this," said Gillian to me as we came barging through the gap for the second time.

"Certainly I don't. Neither does anybody else, however much they may pretend they do."

The only two people who hadn't moved were Aunt Emmy and Roger. They still sat placidly in the same corner while their babies nervously snatched delicious mouthfuls of hedge. Roger grinned and waved at us derisively. He skipped the chestnut filly over to us and said:

"Anybody would think you were at Balaclava, you gallant things you."

"I could slap you, sweet," said Gillian. "Just go away."

Old George's horn now mournfully informed us from the far side that he had given up Kilgarvan and its fox as big as a tiger, and was going on to the famous Speke— a small, compact patch of gorse on the southerly slope of a sheltering hill, half a mile away across the fields, which had never been known not to yield a fox, even if only of normal appearance.

"If we go away down hill from Speke," I said, "poor Andrew won't stand a chance."

"Never mind, he's as happy as a bee at the moment and his nervous system is set in reinforced concrete."

We jogged off in a clattering, chattering cavalcade across the fields to Speke. A slight wind from the north was beginning to blow the rain away and here and there patches of a cold and washy blue showed between the grey, amorphous cloud. It was getting colder.

"Be a hell of a scent this evening," said Mike cheerfully. "Any time ground's hotter'n air you'll see 'em run like stink."

Poodle said darling Mike, so optimistic always, she had thought it *quite* the other way round, Freddy had always said . . .

Any argument about what constitutes good scenting

conditions is inconclusive and not infrequently heated, for somebody has always seen hounds running like stink in weather and over ground that somebody else has proclaimed to be utterly hopeless, might as well go home. Scent is as mysterious as God and causes almost as much controversy among its devotees.

"Oh do look at that terrible horse," said Gillian suddenly.

Paddy Casey's lad had incautiously decided that a canter round might settle his sweating charge, who now swept past us suddenly as if powered by a jet engine, his head nearly on the ground and the lad perched on his withers, trying desperately to stop whilst looking as if he meant to go on—an art that can be seen at its highest on any Irish race course.

"The boy will be quinched," said someone placidly. "That's a horse wouldn't mind himself at all."

Gillian gave a faint squeak and shut her eyes as this prophecy appeared likely to be fulfilled, for the horse was now approaching a narrow, straggly, bramble-topped bank and showed no sign of either abating his pace or allowing himself to be turned from his course. There was a bursting, crashing, catastrophic sound, and he disappeared from view. A few seconds later, undismayed, he and his rider could be seen continuing their career across the further field.

Colonel Wilbraham was hurt and puzzled.

"That's the horse that feller Casey wanted me to buy," he said to me. "Bit unneighbourly, what?"

"A bit," I answered gravely.

Paddy Casey himself now appeared, hastening up alongside us to retrieve the situation. He always rode a thirty-year-old white mare who had long ceased to have any interest in anything except going home.

"I told the lad put him over something for you, Colonel. There's a horse now, would lep Aintree."

"Sure, he'd lep into the Canal then," a muffled voice was heard to exclaim behind us, "for there's no one would turn that felly once he'd be off."

"Oh, aren't they all divine," said Gillian.

Paddy Casey glared reproachfully at her.

We jogged and chattered on across the grey-green fields and all around us, some not far away, some very far, blue, hazy, keeping with arrogant ease their incredible hold upon the heart, were the inevitable mountains that ring the middle of Ireland like the upturned edges of a saucer. One could go away from Kilgarvan, Speke, Kilquin, or any other covert in the West Tipperary country and there, in front of one, would be mountains—perhaps one far, faint peak showing dimly through trees; perhaps a blue and solid range jagged against a cold sky; perhaps a familiar, mighty shoulder humping suddenly up out of the mild plains to make a landmark for lost foxhunters. They are all part of the magic; which, like all good magic, is not easily definable—not to be dissected or labelled Black or White, or distilled successfully into railway posters or guide books. The land is no colour and all colours; drab and sad and achingly beautiful; and whichever it is changes while you try to look at it—for this reason nobody has ever yet painted it with truth; the land keeps its secret.

Everywhere is the haunting sense of nostalgia and poverty and sadness—of things begun and never finished, might have been, wasted, ruined, not even thought about.

Even in the richest grazing lands, where the fattening bullocks move gravely about the fields like heavy princes, there still, are the broken-down, never-to-be-built-up walls; the black-thorn running riot on the rotting banks; the iron bedstead stuck in the gap; the un-openable gates, propped with stones, sagging on rusty hinges; the dusty, pot-holed little roads; the rush-choked ditches and the lame, straying donkeys. Here too, the Big Houses, the square Georgian boxes with their bland façades, their tall, flat windows, their cracked fanlights, their lovely and subtle simplicity, slide gently into ruin—until, as was happening so often at this time, they were rescued by the refugees, disappeared for long months behind a network of scaffolding and re-appeared rain-proof and centrally-heated and perhaps slightly reproving—for had anybody, after all, a right to rescue them; had anybody even bothered to enquire if they wanted to be rescued?

For I think that, perhaps, the closest one may come to analysing the spell of the land is to say that it owes much to the enormous, the subtle and speculative magic of the unsuccessful—and on the damp grey days, the cold blue mornings, the steamy gold evenings, the magic is there, triumphant and unvarying and rather frightening, and the lovely, lonely, ignoble land has you by the heart.

"What are you thinking of?" asked Gillian.

"The mountains."

"Why does one like them so much?"

"I can't imagine."

"But one does, madly."

"Yes."

"I was thinking about Jane and Little Daisy—see them together there, in front of the Wilbrahams—I was thinking how fantastic it is that they should both just be called the same thing—*Women*. There ought to be different names for them."

"There are, sweet."

"Don't be silly—I meant scientifically."

Speke was blank; and so were the faces that turned away from it to begin the mile-long trek down the road to Drumanagh Glen. It was still getting colder, and people were beginning to turn up their coat collars and drop back to look for their cars and sustenance. At the bare and lonely cross-roads some easily-defeated spirits left for home. The Limerick visitors were quietly triumphant and the Pytchley one censorious. Nobody dared speak to old George.

"How about a drink?" asked Gillian. "I see your sweet mother."

The little green car was parked in a gateway up a side road and there was my mother and Richmond, Aunt Emmy, Roger, the babies and Poodle, who was telling my fascinated mother that what everybody was saying about old Dicky was *quite right* and, not only that, but *far worse*.

"Poor old man," said my mother, "if only he'd sack all those terrible servants, nobody would ever know anything."

"I adore your mother," said Gillian. "And how I dislike that dreadful Poodle—she's too pneumatic and too blonde and altogether too fashionable—really, no one who hasn't been to bed with her has any social standing at all."

"You're jealous."

"Of course I am."

She and Poodle greeted each other with delighted cries and Gillian was luckily able to keep her end up with a really hot and fresh piece of gossip, contained in a letter received only that morning (now lying amongst the breakfast litter at Knockmoree having been read and abandoned by Thomas Quin), about who had been seen by whom lunching with who at that quaint Brown's and talking *very earnestly*, "do you think, darling, that that one is breaking up at long last for good and all?"

Gillian often told me sadly in cosier moments how she was always promising herself not to gossip and how she always broke her promises—it was something that was very much on her strange, tough, flexible, and often oddly troubled mind. So now she and the hated Poodle gossiped happily together and drank up what delicious whisky Roger had left, while Richmond leant against the bonnet of the little green car looking noble and courteous, until one of the babies trod heavily on his foot and remained on it. It is a very curious fact about horses— possibly part of their divine silliness that Gillian had noticed; possibly that something inimical in their attitude towards humans that has so often been complained of by those who don't love them—but a fact, certainly—that the most flippant and restless amongst them, having found an agonized human foot to stand on, becomes at once as immovable as a rock.

The baby gazed mildly over Richmond's shoulder, its mind apparently very far away; while its victim clawed unhappily at its chest and knee; while Poodle smartly smacked its quarters with her gloves; while my mother jumped up and down in front of its fixed gaze; while Roger pushed at its shoulder to throw it off its balance and I tried to pull its foot up by main force and Richmond snarled breathlessly:

"*Do* something, damn it—*take the bloody animal off my foot.*"

It was at this rather confused moment that hound voices suddenly rang together like a peal of bells from far down the road.

"Christ!" said Roger, and rocked the baby off Richmond's foot with a last despairing thrust. "Listen!" We stood silent, our eyes popping.

A pause. Then one hound speaking.

"That really *is* Reveller."

Then the triumphant chorus clamouring out again, shaking the cold air. Then the long, wild crying of the horn. The chills began in my spine, the thumping of the blood.

"Oh," said Gillian faintly, "I always feel like that woman in Somerville and Ross, who cried."

Roger seized her ankle and put her up on to the brown animal, who looked suddenly less confidential.

"They must have picked up an outlier—they can't have got to Drumanagh. God help you now if they run away from you."

The voices clamoured on. Nearer? Further? I was up on the grey, although I couldn't remember getting there.

"He's bound to come this way if they're between him and Drumanagh," said Aunt Emmy, her eyes shining. "The wind's right for it and even if it wasn't he'd try to get to Kilgarvan."

The babies swung and wavered about, twittering and sweating and staring all ways at once. Poodle had bolted down the road to her horse. (Even at this enthralling moment Gillian found time to observe that she was the wrong shape for running in breeches.) Someone who had been going home, could be seen galloping back like mad across a far field, amongst jovially bucking bullocks.

Still the voices rang out, gay and confident.

"Wait, wait. Listen."

"I *can't* breathe," said Gillian, faintly.

"*Look!*"

The glowing, dramatic quality of Richmond's voice suited the moment. The fox stood a few yards away, in the middle of the road, staring at us.

"Is it——"

"*Sh-h-h-h-.*"

We froze.

Like a red blown leaf he slipped up the far bank and was gone.

"My God," said Roger. "If we'd headed him I believe old George would have strangled us all with his bare hands. Is he well away, Anthony?"

I moved the grey across the road and stood in my stirrups to see over the bank. My eyes searched the far field. Nothing. The wild spirit had vanished as he had come. Then suddenly, there was the flicker of red-brown again as he passed a gap.

"He's running the wall down to that bloody great ditch at the bottom. I'd say he's making for Kilgarvan all right, and going to cross the point-to-point course."

The voices were faltering slightly.

"Holler, Roger. They'll have to bustle him to get through Kilgarvan."

Roger jumped up on the bank, stuck a finger in his ear and produced a noise of ear-splitting intensity.

"My God!" said Richmond, struck to stone in the road.

Unable to follow the sequence of events, he found the world suddenly going mad around him and was beginning to feel twitchy.

"It's all right," said my mother comfortingly, patting his arm.

Three fields away towards Drumanagh the sound reached old George who, already thinking of Kilgarvan, decided to take a chance on its authenticity. He lifted his lovely, deserving hounds and galloped straight to it.

They came pouring liquidly towards us over a wall and up the field, tense and eager and effortless.

"Oh," said Gillian faintly, "Oh, oh."

I knew exactly what she meant for I was having great difficulty myself with my breathing—something odd seemed to have happened to my solar plexus.

"Where to, Roger?" old George was bawling as he galloped.

Roger was pointing.

"Straight down the wall—making for Kilgarvan."

Hounds flowed around us—the babies were having hysterics—there was grunt and slither and curse—

"Ger-r on, you—*hold* up now"—as old George's wise horse came neatly down into the road and neatly and carefully up and out again over the bigger bank, and now old George was cheering them on to the line under the wall and they owned it at once in a crashing chorus and were off, and Gillian and her brown, who might be confidential, but knew when business was meant, were over and gone after them and I only just managed to keep the grey horse back by turning his head away, until Tommy Dwyer had gone by with one willing, embarrassed tail hound and

then I was landing after him, the grey shaking his head
and behind me the crash and clatter and growing thunder
of hooves and Roger's faint shout of benediction:

"Oh, you lucky b——s." For obviously, this was going
to be altogether too much of a good thing for the babies.

Chapter Eight

On this day, at this time, over this piece of country, Mike's theory about good scenting conditions seemed to be right. Hounds were racing, flinging, driving forward like a dappled cloud. There they went, over the bloody great ditch, leaping, falling short, splashing, scrambling out and on without pausing to shake themselves. There went old George on his neat, wise horse, jumping cleverly, not an inch too far, not a second too soon, his ears cocked. Then Gillian, gloriously leading the field, going at it wildly. I knew that in the last second before the take-off, an expression of ecstatic agony on her face, she would shut her eyes and hang tightly on to a plait of mane, leaving the reins to flap loose, and I was glad that Jane's mare knew her business. Then Tommy Dwyer, still crying encouragement to the tail hound, now streaking just behind old George, a personification of silent, bitter determination to catch up with the pack. Then it was my turn and the grey's stride never seemed to vary, only the dark water, the rushes fleeted suddenly backwards and were gone and he lowered his lean head as we met the steeply rising ground on the far side and his shoulder muscles worked like pistons beneath my knees. Now I was trying to control my wild excitement enough to think which would be the best line to take when we reached the top of the hill, where hounds were driving already over the low wall into the road. It was so long since I had hunted here I had difficulty in visualising the country. Once across the road there would be two or three fields, part of the point-to-point course, sloping gently towards Kilgarvan. But if they got him through the big covert would he swing right or left? On which flank of the pack should I station myself? And what the hell was the wind doing? It seemed to be blowing on my heated face from all directions at once. A snorting horse came up on my right hand, Father Carrigan tucked like a jockey behind its withers on a ragged racing saddle, his eyes gleaming wildly, his spectacles crooked on his nose, his bowler on the back of his head. I sighed inwardly with relief, for Father Carrigan knew the mind of every fox in the country.

"Follow me now, Anthony," he shouted exultantly. "Sure, I know this felly, he wouldn't mind how many miles he'd run. If he can't go down in Kilgarvan he'll go across the bog and make for the hills."

Here he cursed his horse startlingly as it bungled the tiny walls into and out of the road, and streaked away down the big field, half-turned in his saddle to shout advice to me still over his black-clad shoulder.

"Bear right now, Anthony. Follow me. We must jump McCarthy's double where it's sound."

McCarthy's double was the biggest bank in the country. Once I had gone over it on my feet when I was a boy and it was like climbing a minor Alp. I had sprung over the deep wet ditch, alighted about a quarter way up, hauled myself by grass-tuft and root and bramble on to the wide top where there was a beaten path amongst bushes and small trees, crept nervously half-way down the far side and then jumped unsuccessfully out over the six-foot stream and failed to clear it. I had got very wet and Nanny had lectured me.

In the middle of the field, cleared and reinforced, this bank was the official double of the point-to-point course —an enormous, smooth, green hummock, tempting you to jump it and carefully wired up to prevent just such goings-on. In some other places it was unsound, but Father Carrigan would know exactly where to have it. I took a pull and looked for Gillian. She was bearing away left, the silly piece, going down into Kilgarvan with old George and Tommy Dwyer, and she would certainly get lost and left and probably bogged. I yelled despairingly at her and waved furiously and at last she saw me, hesitated, pulled round and came galloping over to me.

"Follow me, you silly woman. Follow Father Carrigan."

We fled together down the gentle slope.

"Jump this exactly where he does. Look—there he goes."

"*Jump this?*"

"Just leave it to the mare."

"Oh—it's too easy."

"Of course it is. You go first. I'll push you off the top if you stick."

"Oh God—why did I *ever* imagine I was an outdoor girl?"

She shut her eyes.

The mare knew exactly what to do and she did it very slowly and deliberately. She looked at the ditch and decided the bottom was sound and waded slowly into it.

"No heroics for me," her behind expressed to my horse, who was dancing with impatience. She then reared herself straight up with a wallowing noise, like a sea-monster, and arrived at the top of the bank in two heaving bounds which slightly loosened Gillian, even though she had a different plait in each hand. They disappeared from my view and there was a series of sliding sounds and then a heavy thump. I could not see them, but I knew exactly what the mare had done. She had clambered carefully half-way down, just as I had done on my feet, and had then paused, waving her head and neck at the stream like an elephant testing something with its trunk and shifting her hind-legs carefully to see if she had a firm take-off, while Gillian crouched nervelessly in her saddle with popping eyes, swallowing. Then she had jumped out and over it, just far enough and no further.

"Are you out of the way?" I shouted.

A faint, wordless shriek of assent came back to me. Just as the grey started at it I was aware of Mike Harrington on his chestnut coming as if he was going into the last at Sandown and I thought, "They'll both be killed without a doubt." Then the grey was up and changing and over and out with a wonderful feeling of freedom and ease and effortless timing, so that for a second I saw myself on him, as Aunt Emmy did, "tipping the double like a Punchestown horse" leading the field in the Hunt Cup—but only for a second.

Hounds were chiming away confidently down in Kilgarvan, and were obviously running hard through it. Father Carrigan had disappeared from my view but Gillian was galloping down the field in a determined manner that indicated she knew where he had gone. I set off after her, glancing uneasily back over my shoulder—for Mike was obviously going to be on the ground in a minute and supposing there was nobody else coming that way to pick him up? I wrestled unhappily with my conscience and the grey horse raked angrily at my uncertain hands and said "For God's sake let's *go*." And then Mike and his chestnut appeared behind us, apparently soaring down from the sky, and turned a complete somersault before they hit the ground.

I very much regret having to record that my sole feeling as I pulled my horse round, was one of fury. I was going to miss what looked like an excellent hunt because Mike chose to ride a crazy racehorse over a country where what was needed was a cross between a pony and a panther. As I trotted back to them the horse thrashed uncertainly to its feet, looked round vaguely, saw Gillian's mare and made off down the field at full gallop, inextricably entangled in its reins. But Mike remained on the ground. And then like an answer to prayer, something altogether too good to be true, O excellent, cosy, capable, self-sacrificing man, Dr. Paddy Herlihy from Garnagarry came slipping down off the bank on Mick O'Connor's pony that drew a cart to the creamery when it wasn't hunting.

He pulled up and dismounted in sad resignation, his pug-like face puckered.

"Couldn't I see what would happen a field away? Not the thrack of a heel did the horse lay to it, only knocked back at it with his tail—was it hurdling, God help us, he thought he was at? And I to have my first hunt for a fortnight, with the 'flu that's about."

I hovered helpfully, and he looked up at me, from where he was poking gently at Mike, and grinned.

"Get away on to them, then, you. What good that we'd both miss it? Sure, he's only winded and there's a dozen felly's about with dogs that can help me instead of confusing the hunt."

With enormous relief and a certain amount of shame, I hustled the willing grey off down the field. At the bottom was a sticky gap jammed with thorny bushes. I jumped it and heard hounds very close and swung right through an open gateway and there were Gillian and Father Carrigan, that first-class reader of foxy minds, breathing heavily and trying to hold their shifting horses still, while fifty yards away hounds went streaming and singing across the field in front of us.

"Oh, oh," said Gillian to me, with shining eyes, her stock under one ear and both leathers twisted where she had lost her irons over the double and jammed her feet back into them in a carefree manner.

"Didn't I tell you," shouted Father Carrigan triumphantly. "Sharp right he turned out of Kilgarvan and he's for the hills this minute."

"Have you seen Brigadier Harrington's horse?" I asked him.

"I have, and he wouldn't let us lay a finger on him—he's gone in to McCarthy's yearlings below—sure, McCarthy'll catch him when he'd settle."

"Have you seen Mike?" Gillian asked me.

"I have, indeed, and the doctor from Garnagarry is with him now."

"Oh, poor Mike—is he all right?"

"Not very."

"Oh, Anthony, how can you be so heartless?"

"I feel like a character in Nimrod—the pace was too good to enquire. Come on, now."

For old George had gone by, scrubbing his wise horse that wouldn't gallop unless the necessity was stark and Tommy Dwyer had gone by with a purple, intent face and as we set off again two or three toiling figures were coming up from Kilgarvan—I looked back and thought I saw Hubert and the roan mare, Jane Harrington and a couple of unidentifiable forms behind them.

"Where's Andrew?" I shouted to Gillian as we galloped along the rutty headland with Father Carrigan, all rebounding off each other from time to time in a not very controlled manner. Her answer which seemed to contain the words "little brute" was lost to me in the confusion that ensued at the next gap, where Father Carrigan's horse, who was slightly leading as we came to it, resolutely refused to jump a timber rail jammed across it that could not have been much more than eighteen inches high, coming to a jarring halt with a swerve that sent its rider down its shoulder. Gillian always said afterwards that she had heaved him back into the saddle by his respectable black breeches, but all I can remember is Father Carrigan pulling out of our way with a despairing cry of "Holy God!" and sending his now willing horse scrambling over the bank, which was about twelve feet high, very narrow, extremely slippery and crowned with jagged broken tree stumps.

I reflected, as I looked back at him, on what a pity it was that his horse and Mike's could not somehow manage to combine their respective talents.

We pounded on. The banks were becoming wide, low slippery humps, with big ditches full of water—we were approaching the bog. Here we would cross it at its narrowest part—about a mile—and then if we were lucky find ourselves in an excellent part of the country; grazing grounds with big, sound banks and small walls. "The hills" which Father Carrigan had referred to was really *a* hill—Slievemore, the big blue shoulder rising out of the plain, with the dark, shifting cloud shadows fleeting across its bulk, and the low, ragged clouds themselves lying now across its peak in banks which the freshening wind was beginning to blow away.

"See where's he's making for," I called to Gillian.

"If only I could breathe," was her response, the brown mare plugging determinedly on beside me, her head low, delighted with her breathless and light and unmasterful rider, and confident in her own power to get there, wherever it might be. Behind us came Father Carrigan, still bitterly lecturing his non-timber-jumper, and behind him, apparently, still no one else at all. We pulled to a walk to slide down an extremely steep, short slope, at the bottom of which we would jump a huddle of stones pretending to be a wall, and find ourselves on the bog-road.

"Are we leading the field?" gasped Gillian as we slithered down towards it.

"Pounded 'em."

"Oh . . . *fascinating*. . . . Do I look at all like Dick Christian?"

"Not really."

"Oh . . . I so hoped I did. . . . I've never done such a thing before."

Hounds went fleeting like a blizzard across the bog, old George and Tommy Dwyer battering at a shameless gallop up the road after them.

"Oh," said Gillian, as we landed together on to it, "their poor glass legs will never stand it."

I thought it more than probable. But there was nothing else to be done. There was goat-nibbled turf at the sides of the road, but there were deep, irregular ditches cut into it at frequent intervals, tiring and dangerous to horse and rider. Anyone who has tried to gallop a horse on a grass verge will know what a great penchant they have for the hard, high road in spite of their poor glass legs and how they will bend and lurch and pull sideways towards it, refusing to look where they are going until they get their way, and the unique sensation of galloping on a hard, clattering surface.

"Anyway, it's not slippery," said Gillian hopefully, as we fled along, scattering stones, lurching in and out of ruts and making a noise like a hundred Crusaders charging in armour, "but I couldn't feel guiltier, could you?"

Certainly I couldn't. Would the grey horse, I wondered, be lamed for life? But still the pace was too good to enquire. We must gallop or hounds would run away from us, so we galloped, guilty or not.

There was a broken-down cabin a little way on and from out of it slipped two lurchers, oblivious of shouted curses from within, to race, shrieking and nipping at the heels of old George's horse who, endeavouring to kick back at them as it galloped, very nearly came down. Old George's scream of execration and the pistol-cracks of his and Tommy Dwyer's thongs sent them howling and cowering into the ditch, from where they launched a further attack on us, while at the same time two apparently idiot children ran gaily out under our horse's feet. Their mother, incredibly tangled-looking and quite oblivious to their fate, hung over the half-door of their home and screamed harshly, hadn't she seen the fox himself and the dogs too ahead of us and they never stopping to draw breath?

Neither did we draw breath, not then or for some time after. It was a fearful moment. I shall never know exactly what the grey horse did, but he managed somehow not to lay the thrack of a heel on those undeserving brats—presumably he knocked back at them with his tail. Gillian's mare appeared to rise straight into the air in a sort of confused *fouetté*—her feet working on nothing. Then we were past.

"I can't look back," chattered Gillian.

I did so, with dread. The children, undismayed, were just jumping gaily under Father Carrigan's horse—who became so unnerved and so muddled with its feet that it ended up wallowing in the ditch, with the lurchers in hysterics around it. Benediction flowed from the Father in an unending stream as they struggled out again. Gillian always swore that he had laid about the children with his whip, but I am ready to believe that this was artistic license on her part, for Father Carrigan, wild though he might be in appearance and behaviour, was the soul of kindness.

Now he came clattering on again behind us, talking angrily to himself and suddenly behind him again there was an eager hooting and, looking back, I saw my mother remorselessly driving the groaning little green car with Richmond hanging out of the window as if chasing gangsters in a rather bad film. On one step clung somebody in pink (Mike? Colonel Wilbraham? The Pytchley?) and on the other—could it be?—it surely must be the tangled and unmaternal figure from the cabin. Around the back wheels the indefatigable lurchers nipped and shrieked once again, and further back, running nobly but rather hopelessly, wreathed in smelly clouds from the exhaust came the abandoned children. And then, far, far, far behind, just coming down on to the road, four or six or so more conventional figures, correctly mounted and no doubt absolutely furious.

The grey cannoned heavily off Gillian's mare.

"Oh, do, *do* look where you're going, Anthony."

"Oh, Lord," I said, bending on the grey's neck.

"You're ill!" said Gillian, pallidly.

"No. But I've just seen Mama and Richmond with that terrible woman from the cabin."

"Where? Where?"

"Not very far behind us."

"I *can't* look. I daren't. If I start laughing now I'm finished." She stared desperately ahead with a fixed face.

We were coming off the bog. The road was ceasing to have the appearance of a causeway and was tending to sink between thorn-crowned banks and become a boreen. We could hear hounds off on our left and bearing away.

"We must get out of here at the next jumpable place," I said to Gillian.

Then we turned a sharp, downhill corner and fell slap on to old George and Tommy Dwyer, who were penned up facing an enormous, enthralled horse who was drawing a cart that just fitted the boreen. A small boy gesticulated helplessly from where he was sitting on the near shaft.

"Back," roared old George to him in a Jehovah voice. "Back, damn it, *back*!"

The boy stood up obediently and leaned heavily on the

reins with the whole weight of his meagre body. The horse opened its mouth very wide, stuck its neck straight out and advanced towards us with an eager, welcoming sound.

"Sweet Christ," said old George hoarsely.

"Oh, *darling*," said Gillian to me with tears in her eyes. "*Do* something. Make a hole in that."

"That" was the high and healthy and thick growth of blackthorn that crowned the bank on our left. The bank itself was not very high, but it looked slippery and rotten and the take-off out of the boreen was appalling.

"And the grandest gate you ever saw only just down from us!" wailed Tommy Dwyer.

He backed his horse and turned and booted him into the bank. Both were game but the thorns made a quick, clean jump impossible and as the horse dwelt the bank gave way immediately under his floundering feet. For a long few seconds he thrashed like a stranded whale above us. He was going to fall, but would he fall over or back into the lane? Tommy had slipped neatly off his back and was perched, like an anxious robin amongst the thorns, clutching the end of the reins. The horse gave one final desperate kick and disappeared from our view, sliding on his stomach. Tommy leapt after him into space. There was a hideaous squelching sound.

"They'll be into the boggy dyke beyond for sure," the small boy remarked conversationally.

Old George gave him a brimstone look. Suddenly the boy's face became illuminated with an idea.

"Wait while I'd run down and get the slasher for you."

He leapt up and disappeared down the boreen. The

abandoned horse and cart moved further into the fearful mêlée.

"Tommy, are you clear, damn you?" bawled old George.

"Wait now, wait, sir."

There were flounderings, and urging noises and then the encouraging cry "Come on now sir, but sure 'tis a grave you have to lep, 'tis a fearful place altogether."

Old George set his purple jaw and lepped. I hung desperately on to the cart horse who had a strong notion of lepping himself.

Old George and his horse went the same way as Tommy and his—with the difference that old George was not spry enough to nip off. They rolled together out of sight.

"He'll be killed," said Gillian, faintly. "Why do we like doing this?"

Crash. Flounder. Squelch. And then a slightly shaken bawl:

"Come on then, you two."

I wrestled strongly with the cart horse.

"Listen, Gillian, don't have it. It's a bloody awful place. Give it up."

I felt a sharp panic for her, she looked so small suddenly. Her lips folded obstinately. Apparently she was still feeling like Dick Christian. The brown mare cocked her ears and seemed to take a deep breath.

They had it, determinedly. Old George said afterwards that even at that flustering moment, with his hounds running away from him every second, with his own horse still on the ground trying to get its breath back, with the winded Tommy Dwyer's whole weight on him as he tried to put him up; even so he was struck to stone by the sight of Gillian's arrival. She came with her eyes shut. She had abandoned her reins altogether and clung tightly with both hands to the pommel of her saddle. The mare made a wonderful effort, hit the edge of the "grave" and tipped up. She ploughed on her head for a few yards and then righted herself, blowing mud triumphantly from her nostrils, with her bridle on the ground and her rider still in the saddle.

"I declare to my God", Tommy Dwyer was wont to say, in describing this feat afterwards, which he did very often, "there's not a jock in the country, no not J. J. himself, would have stayed above the way Mrs. Lodwick did, and the mare walking on her head the way she might be in a circus."

But now it was my turn and the grey's. The expression "riding for a fall" is very easily used and has a dashing ring about it—actually to do such a thing, however, arouses a feeling of sick anticipation comparable only to that experienced at the moment when the dentist's hand reaches for the drill.

We were not only going to fall, I felt, but there was also nothing to prevent the cart and horse from falling on top of us, since the horse was abviously feeling ambitious and there was no one to curb his feelings once I had gone. I belaboured him rather hopelessly with my whip until he gave way sufficiently to allow us a little room. My heart and stomach had changed places as the grey heaved himself up into the thorny gap, with everything giving way at once under his clever feet. But I need not have worried. The grey had brains and he decided instantly that, with no firm take-off, any attempt to jump the boggy dyke beyond would end in failure. Instead he dropped lightly and neatly and deliberately down into it and heaved himself out again, light and neat still, and shook himself with a noise like thunder all over old George's horse, which at once got to its feet indignantly.

"By God, that's a clever horse of Emmy's," said old George. "My b—— just lost his head."

He was clasping Gillian's mare's naked face delicately to his chest by nose and ear while Tommy Dwyer endeavoured to pick up her bridle, much hampered by his horse who had decided that the bridle was alive, and was refusing to go near it. I jumped off and took his horse and old George's while they restored to Gillian a measure of control and then I put them both up, and by that time I was so breathless with fright and exhaustion that I really thought I should lose the hunt yet through sheer physical inability to get up on the grey again. But Tommy Dwyer leant from his saddle and heaved nobly and I was aboard again and flying, for the grey had breathed himself nicely—there was agonizing mud in my right eye and I could not find my irons for the moment but ahead was good grass and sound banks—and behind a piteous, lonely, beseeching scream. I looked back. The cart horse stood reared up with his forefeet on the bank, imploring us to return.

We fled on, through two delicious gateways without gates.

"Where's Father Carrigan?" Gillian shouted breathlessly.

Where indeed? I had forgotten him. I looked back. Nobody. He had been close behind us coming off the bog, and it was not like Father Carrigan to lose a good start. Nor had he, for as I looked forward again, across the country that was now beginning to rise slightly as we went towards Sleivemore, there was the familiar crouched dark back, slipping along at least two fields ahead of us all.

"How did he get there?"

"God knows."

"That damned priest," growled old George, "he's always ahead of me, blast his Papist soul."

Old George was well known never to have entered a church since he had left Eton, but in the presence of Roman Catholicism his Protestantism was relentless and militant. He preferred, he said, his own type of damnation.

Old George's horse was tiring now; at the next bank he misjudged his distance and nearly fell back. Gillian's mare had a slight roll in her stride as we crossed the next field. I was frankly exhausted but the grey horse was going on as light as thistledown, his ears cocked still, still reaching for each jump eagerly, and I tried to sit as quiet as possible and not hinder him, even if I could not help him. There came a wall on to a cart-track, with a stone-faced bank out of it. Old George's horse came to his knees over the wall, slithered and scuffled and heaved and stopped with his chest against the bank, his head hanging over it and his tail stretched out, quivering.

"He's beat," said old George. "The b——. He's old, like me."

He ran his hand lovingly down the wet shoulder.

"Get on to them, Tommy, damn you. What the hell are you hanging about for?"

Tommy got on, with slither and slip and clatter, into a herd of young bullocks who wallowed excitedly with him down the field, ponderously playful.

"Get on, you two," said old George. He had got off

and was loosening his horse's girths, his head hidden under the saddle flap so that his voice was muffled.

He didn't want us to see his face. "Oh, hell," I thought, "hell," and got off the grey and plucked George's reins from his hand.

"Get up quick—he's a bottomless horse."

Honour and glory for Aunt Emmy, anyway. Old George's face, taken from beneath the saddle flap, was even purpler than usual.

"I shouldn't do it to you, Anthony."

"Don't be a fool."

I pitched him up. My leathers were much too long— he crossed them over the pommel of the saddle and was gone, the grey jumping out big over the slight drop. Gillian looked woefully at me before she followed.

"Oh, darling, the *chivalry*. Roger need never speak about Round Tables again."

Then she, too, was gone. There was the slap and thunder of their hooves and the bawling of the bullocks. Then silence, except for the heavy panting of old George's horse. Silence? Yes, silence. I strained my ears, but I could not hear hounds. And they had only been two or three fields ahead of us. A check? Had they over-run in this poached, bullock-foiled field? If so, there was hope for me yet. I turned the horse's head to the wind and earnestly exhorted him to breathe deeply which he did without hesitation. Then I heard Tommy Dwyer's voice not very far away raised in gentle encouragement to his hounds. Undoubtedly a check. And yet, what hope could there really be for me, since the fox was bound to be forward if he was making for Sleivemore? Or had he thought up something very tricky as he ran through the bullocks? I clambered to the top of the bank and looked about me. The field directly to the right of the one which the bullocks were in, ran increasingly boggily down to a narrow stream. Had he gone to cross it, the old customer, the cunning Charles James, running first in the middle of the bullocks and then turning sharply at a right angle off his point? If so, he would now be slipping at ease along the far bank, looking for a suitable place to re-cross it and point again for the haven of Sleivemore. As I cogitated and still no hound spoke, the little green car came roaring indomitably towards me and lurched to a standstill with its curious load.

"Anthony," said my mother serenely, peering out at me. "That's not Emmy's horse."

"I know," I said.

"Then where *is* Emmy's horse?"

Before I could answer there was another diversion— a clapping and flapping and thudding and a loose horse landing over the wall into our midst, wild-eyed, mud on its saddle, a leather gone and broken reins. My heart leapt up as I beheld it to be Conor Molloy's horse. It slithered up to old George's horse and blew on it in a friendly "Thank-goodness-I've-found-someone-at-last" manner. Old George's horse laid back its ears and bit the newcomer smartly on the shoulder just to show it its place.

"You hold this one," said my mother sweetly to Richmond, pressing the broken rein into his hand with the air of someone distributing favours to the gentlemen at a charity ball. Richmond's hand closed, nervelessly, on it. He appeared to be speechless and was obviously strongly affected, but in what way I was not quite certain.

"Have the dogs the fox ate?" enquired the careless mother from the cabin.

"They have not, then," I answered in the idiom.

"Where are they, Anthony? Oh, I forgot this is Colonel Bowser, he's staying with Poodle. [The Pytchley collar looked sharply defensive and fingered his stock.] And they're coming to have a drink with us tonight, that is, of course, if we can find her—or anyone—where *is* everyone, anyway?"

"All I know is that George has got Aunt Emmy's horse and he and Tommy and Gillian and Father Carrigan are over there—they seem to have checked and I think they probably over-ran it through those bullocks. I haven't seen anyone else at all, except as we came across the bog I thought perhaps I saw Jane and Poodle, a long way back."

"Nearly everybody went to the left around Kilgarvan, that's what happened and they got thrown out and they haven't caught up yet." She looked back over the wall. "Here's somebody now."

It was Caroline. The Araby little horse, black with sweat, landed neatly and jauntily beside us and tossed its head rudely at the other two. Caroline's smile was enchanting, her face creamy under the mud-splashes, her velvet eyes glowing.

"Thank heaven I found somebody at last—I do hate following hoof marks. Where are they? Why have you got my father's horse, Anthony?"

Oh, noble, pure and unselfish motive thus happily turned to glorious gain! I explained.

"How *very* kind of you. Listen, I'll tell you what you can do. Change bridles and get up on Conor's horse."

"Oh, yes, Anthony," said my mother. "You mustn't miss it now." She was already divesting George's horse of its bridle. "Just take hold of an ear, would you, Mr. Kerr. That's right, he won't try and move."

But he did. For at that very instant the ringing, the clamour, broke again on the air and the triumphant twanging of old George's horn. My thumb was in Conor's horse's mouth as it mumbled angrily at the strange and frothy bit, refusing to take it.

"Oh, hurry, hurry," wailed Caroline, in a frenzy. "Oh, listen to them, the darlings—hurry, hurry."

Old George's horse, breathed and rid of the weight and highly indignant at the strange turn of affairs, twitched his ear away from Richmond, jumped the bank with a grunt and was away, the saddle slowly sliding round under his belly as he went.

"I told you to hold his ear, Mr. Kerr," said my mother, mildly.

I twisted my thumb madly in Conor's horse's mouth, jammed in the bit, pulled the bridle with an effort over his ears—it was too tight for the poor brute—and left the throat-latch dangling as Poodle's boy-friend bent to give me a leg-up; a noble lift that nearly sent me clean over the big horse—the Pitchley back, I saw as he bent, was smeared with mud from collar to skirt.

I am very glad that there exists no photograph of myself jumping that bank on Conor's horse. I think my head was somewhere near his tail as we landed and I can remember seeing my hands raised in front of me as if in prayer. Then we were scudding away after Caroline and from somewhere not so very far ahead, once again unfaltering, the glorious voices came back to us.

I have no very clear recollection of the rest of that hunt. I realised at once that I had no hope of holding Conor's horse, who seemed to be as fresh as a daisy, and was taking delighted advantage of the mild half-moon snaffle that had replaced his own twisted one. He was big and awkward, green and hot, and his jumping was slapdash, to say the least of it. No thought of refusing ever entered his head, he went gaily and gallantly into his fences with ears cocked, but with no very clear-cut idea as to what he was going to do about them. He had great panache, but all his decisions were made in mid-air. Twice he was nearly down—more times than I care to remember I was nearly off. I was riding without stirrups, since one is no good to anybody, and I was getting very tired. I gave him his head and prayed and once or twice adopted Gillian's expedient of shutting my eyes. We passed Caroline, who shouted something happily to me, we passed Father Carrigan, whose horse was reduced to a toiling jog, "God help us, Anthony, what horse have you now?"

Half a field ahead Gillian's brown mare was doggedly cantering, rolling like the *Queen Mary* in a heavy sea, and ahead again, forging further, jumping cleanly still, the game grey horse carried old George to his hounds.

"By God," I thought momentarily, "I *will* win the Hunt Cup on him."

The land was rising ever more steeply, the wide green fields, the sound banks giving way to rough, tussocky little enclosures, patchworked by little, crumbling walls. Sleivemore, enormous in the fading light, bulked silent and close above us, shutting out the pallid evening sky. We were coming on to its lower slopes. At the next wall Gillian's mare's heels waved in the air, she tipped up and crumpled amongst the tussocky grass. I landed near them.

"Oh, darling, *heavens*, what horse have you got now—did you see us fall?—do, *do* go on, quick. I'll just wait until this poor honey gets her breath—I see Father Carrigan coming—do, *do* go on."

Now, as I went, I saw hounds again for the first time since we had crossed the bog, driving across a low ridge above and to the left of me. They had had a view, I thought, for the high screaming for blood had come into their voices. After them the grey horse slipped like a ghost. Conor's horse lowered his head to climb, picking his way on the rocky outcrop. We came up with Tommy Dwyer limping, leading his beaten horse, almost in tears.

"Sure, don't they deserve him, if hounds ever did? But he'll get into the rocks above and then he can run the whole inside of the hill—the bloody place is hollow—who'd ever think they'd bring him to here from Drumanagh?"

"Never mind, Tommy—it must be a twelve-mile point—you've given us all something to talk about."

But Tommy was thinking of his hounds. Conor's horse slid and slithered.

"Best get off now, sir, 'tis a dreadful place for a tired horse."

When I did so I went to my knees. My legs seemed to be made of cotton-wool, and my feet to have no connection with the rest of me. I was not quite sure where I was putting them and I staggered along drunkenly. Away in front, abruptly, the voices died. Then they clamoured again, but singly, brokenly, mournfully, informing us of frustration and a thirst unassuaged. Old George's horn told us the same and round the spine of the ridge we came upon them, a little above us, milling and crying around the great earth in the rocks, the grey horse standing amongst them, his head drooping at last, and old George's face glowing like a lantern through the deepening dusk.

"By God, they nearly had him, the darlings, they were running right into him—ten yards more, five even and he wouldn't have made it."

"A good fox," I said. "A marvellous run, George. You've made history to-day. Congratulations."

"And only the locals up," said old George with immense satisfaction. "Leave him, leave him now, my darlings. Count 'em, Tommy—I think they were all on."

"Here comes one non-local," I said, as Gillian came plodding up towards us, trailing Jane's mare, like a tired child dragging a balloon away from a party. Behind her came Caroline and Father Carrigan, both also on foot. Father Carrigan seemed to have caught old George's horse and was leading it by the thong of his whip looped round its throat. The old horse lifted his head and whinnied in a throaty murmur when he saw hounds.

We stood around idly, enveloped in an immense tiredness and content. Old George and Tommy were murmuring endearments to their lovely hounds as they counted them and pulled thorns out of sore pads.

There was a smell of sweating horses and the evening wind, and a star was out above Sleivemore. Old George put the horn to his lips for the last time and blew the long, heartrending "Home".

Chapter Nine

Sunny Sunday morning in the uneven, cobbled old stable-yard at Knockmoree. A wind, soft, slight and from the west, just lifted my hair as I sat on the edge of the old-fashioned stone drinking trough and inhaled the first, the most perfect cigarette. The smoke eddied gently away. Quite soon it would rain, but at the moment the day was without flaw.

There was a steady munching, a shifting, a sighing, an occasional ringing stamp from the horses all round me, invisible in their boxes, happily occupied with their morning hay. From the small inner yard where the brood mares lived came the clatter of bucket handles. Matty and his underlings had gone off to Mass, driven in the little green car by the steward, and Roger was giving the aristocratic matrons their skim milk before they were turned out to graze.

"Oh, what a beautiful morning," he sang in a soft, off-key baritone. "Oh, what a beautiful day," and following some train of thought hidden to me, changed abruptly to "La vie en rose". I wondered which the mares appreciated more. Presently he appeared leading two of the sleek, bulging, dignified ladies, their tongues still working round their milky noses, their unshod feet treading delicately on the cobbles. When they saw me sitting innocently on the trough enjoying the morning, the divine silliness of their kind overcame them at once. They stopped dead and threw up their heads—signalling wildly to each other, "Look out, here's a panther!" Their cocked ears met at the tip in excitement and their soft eyes shone and bulged.

"Come along now," said Roger to them comfortingly. "It's only Anthony working out the last act."

They sidled suspiciously past, curving their bodies sideways in case I should suddenly put out a paw.

"You've given them a fright," said Roger reprovingly. "Suppose the foals come out looking like playwrights— Aunt Emmy *will* be cross." He wandered on, out under the archway towards the paddocks in front of the house where all the mares spent their dreamy days. He looked tired, which was hardly surprising, since he had been drunk for the past three days. And I felt tired, in spite of the benediction of the morning, for too much had been happening. I had come home intending quietly to wrestle with a difficult piece of writing, quietly to marry Gillian and possibly—although of this I felt there had never really been much hope—to recover what little peace of mind I had ever had; to look simply at simple things like horses, mountains, rooks and rain and thus to unwind myself a little. And now the subtle simplicity of Ireland, the let-things-slide, the *mañana* and time-enough and be easy were only winding me tighter and into more complicated coils.

I had never yet looked at the play, and Richmond had never mentioned it. This I thought sinister to an alarming degree, for, much as I dreaded the spiritual wrestling match that must inevitably ensue, I dreaded more the idea, daily more certain in my mind, that Richmond never would mention the play again, that Richmond's dragon-fly enthusiasms were at the moment hovering scintillatingly over Ireland and over Knockmoree and that he was going to require me to hover in just such a manner and produce a new, a thrilling, a down-to-earth effort, loud with the clamour of the West Tipperary foxhounds, that would have the weary first-nighters whooping in the stalls. Only too clearly, I thought, I could see his mind working towards it—but if I had seen only a little further, just a little more clearly at that moment, I would not have rested in such comparative peace on the stone water-trough while Aunt Emmy took Richmond to look at a horse she thought might suit him.

"On Sunday morning?" Richmond had asked at breakfast, as Aunt Emmy proposed it.

"The very best moment we could choose, sure. The owner will be at Mass, for certain."

"But won't we want to see the owner?"

"Not until we've had a quiet look at the horse—ah, you'll learn yet. You'll need gum-boots—he's in a dreadful boggy field."

Richmond had gone quietly, happily drowning in Aunt Emmy's glorious aura of ease, surrounded by the madly excited Labradors.

"But can he ride, would you know?" Gillian had asked.

"God knows—you know a little detail like that wouldn't bother Aunt Emmy for an instant."

"But where will he keep it? Just in the stalls, I suppose?"

"Here, I expect. Probably Aunt Emmy has told him to keep popping over between rehearsals while she gets it ready for Punchestown."

"*This* year?"

"Or next. Aunt Emmy doesn't take much account of years. It's her most powerful charm."

"She's altogether a very undermining woman," Gillian had said. "I've never known Richmond's ego kept under so long."

And even Richmond, it seemed at the moment, was the least of the problems. There was Roger, who had arrived back so very drunk on the day of the great run from Drumanagh, that Hester had gone straight to bed announcing that she was miscarrying and ordering the steward to go for the doctor at once.

"Although miscarry, my lady," Nanny had said firmly to my mother, "is not what Mrs. Hubert is anywhere near and I'd hold to what I say if the King himself said otherwise."

These were strong words indeed, for in Nanny's view the King himself was only very slightly less reliable than the Almighty.

"Oh dear," my mother had said, when we arrived home that night, stiff, tired, delighted with ourselves and babbling endlessly and no doubt boringly, of the hunt—only to find Roger passed out on the drawing-room sofa, hovered over by the horrified and delighted Thomas Quin—"Oh dear, I *do* rather blame Emmy for letting him go home alone, with all those dreadful little places between here and Drumanagh—seven at least—Emmy must have been mad—I do wonder where she is—Anthony, dear, do just run out to the stables and see to the filly because there wouldn't have been anyone there when they got back."

(Roger and Aunt Emmy had planned to ride their

babies back and let Matty and Micky just bring the other three horses.)

But the filly had been warm and dry, rugged up and deep in her feed and not at all pleased to see me. She poked absently at me with a hind leg, and went on eating. I could imagine how Roger, more and more slow and wavering and deliberate, had held sternly on to himself while the routine had been gone through; the mechanical motions, one by one, struggled with and finished until, at last, with the rugs on, the chilled water drunk, the feed mixed, he could let himself go into the golden oblivion— only the mud-splashed saddle and bridle that could not be harmed by his neglect, lay in a tangle outside the box. As I contemplated them Aunt Emmy rode cosily into the yard in the near-dark and I went to hold the baby as she lowered herself ungracefully off it.

"I went home with Euphemia Coke—her horse had over-reached—I'd been wanting for ages to see her year-lings, and then we had tea. Tell me now, Anthony, did you have a great hunt?"

"We did, Aunt Emmy, the hunt of the century, we ended up on Sleivemore and Roger's had a wonderful time too, and he's ended up on the sofa, luckily."

"Oh, *dear*—wasn't that very silly of me now?"

"It was, rather."

It turned out afterwards that Roger had not come home alone, but with Paddy Casey, who had heard him talking to his lad at the meet, and was bent on revenge. So really there did seem to be some excuse for Roger—but not according to Hubert, who sat bursting with anger and protection by Hester's bedside and said really, this sort of thing simply could not go on, it was wanton, that's all, why couldn't Roger do some work and stop disgracing everybody.

"But Hubert, darling," said my mother, gently, "he isn't disgracing anybody, or hurting anybody except himself."

Hubert snorted.

When Thomas Quin and I had put Roger to bed I went wearily to have a bath and found Gillian had forestalled me, lying back in the usual cloud of steam and Mary Chess, blissful, with eyes shut and red patches on the insides of her knees. I sat heavily on the edge of the bath and she opened her eyes.

"Darling—you haven't even got your boots off."

"No."

"Are you worried about Roger?"

"Only if people are going to bully him."

"Hester?"

"Hester's miscarrying."

"Balls."

"I expect you're right. Hester, or Hubert or both. They'll bully him and Roger will be very contrite and agree with every word they say, and he'll be so upset he'll go on a blind for a week. He's very twitchy when he comes round always and it nearly sends him off his head to be bullied then."

"Couldn't we guard him?"

"That's what we must do—let me into that bath now and tell Thomas Quin to give us tea and eggs."

Before I went down to the tea and eggs I looked at Roger. He was still out cold—I could hear voices murmuring seriously in the next room where the doctor was with Hester. My mother came out of it and very nearly winked at me, only not quite in case it should be unfair.

"What does the doctor say?" I asked coldly.

"That she's upset and overwrought."

"The bitch."

"Anthony darling, please try and be more charitable. I know it's very difficult."

"Not for you, my little one. But you know she's only working to get Roger out of here."

My mother sighed and looked suddenly very old and even smaller than usual. I remembered that she had had a very long and exhausting day.

"Never mind." I kissed her. "Come and have some tea."

The wonderful eggs, the long, long draughts of dangerously hot, whisky-laced tea, the buttered toast, the relaxation, the roaring fire, the soft lights and colourings, the magnificent re-telling of the hunt to Aunt Emmy, proved all too seductive and to my everlasting shame I forgot about Roger until my mother said suddenly, as we lay back in unbuttoned attitudes:

"Is Hubert having tea upstairs?"

And then it was too late. For Hubert, urged on by Hester, had gone and sat on Roger's bed and had pounced on him when he came round, bewildered and miserable, and told him that Hester's life and the child's life were in danger because of him and that nobody would stand for his nonsense any longer. So it was that when I roused myself from my selfish daze at my mother's question and went out into the hall to go upstairs I met Roger staggering down them with Hubert close behind him, still lecturing.

". . . and I can tell you this, I've read books on the subject and it's only because you want to draw attention to yourself—you want to make yourself interesting—that's all it is."

"F—— that," said Roger thickly, and lurched into the dining-room, where he began to clatter aggressively amongst the decanters.

"Hubert," said my mother, who had come quickly out of the drawing-room. "You must be famished—do go and have some tea and I'll see to Roger."

"Did you hear the language he's using, mother?"

"No."

"It's most unsuitable."

For what? I longed to ask, but my mother was throwing me a pleading look.

"You two go and finish tea", I said, "and I'll deal with Roger."

Hubert was drawn away, glowering suspiciously, into the drawing-room. Roger was pouring himself a very large glass of whisky, with a shaking hand. He turned upon me at once, tragic and furious.

"So you'll b-bloody deal with me, will you? You're going to s-see to me, are you? God damn you, take your interfering face away. I'm not a hound-puppy that's made a mess in the b-bloody house."

Gillian appeared suddenly beside me.

"Come on, Roger, sweet. We'll all come and have a party in your room. Bring the bottle."

He had looked at her and begun to weep.

*　　*　　*　　*　　*

Much later that night Gillian said to me:

147

"I can't help very slightly worrying about Andrew. I do so wonder where he is."

"With Jane, of course."

"And Mike, still unconscious, do you suppose?"

"They're probably all unconscious by now."

"Oh, dear."

"Darling, you mustn't let being a mother get you down."

"I do try not to."

*　　　*　　　*　　　*　　　*

Later still Andrew arrived back, driven in the Cadillac by Mike's groom. He put his head round the drawing-room door at us with a smug look. He was almost literally licking his lips. He said good-night and went stumping away.

"Oh, the little beast," said Gillian fondly. "He's still got his boots on."

"And what do you suppose *that* proves?"

"Nothing, I'm afraid." She sighed heavily.

"I don't know what you're fussing about. Jane couldn't be better for him. She won't let him take himself seriously and she's not expensive."

"Oh, you're so catty." But she still looked slightly woebegone. Presently she said inconsequently, "Do you think Jane looks older than me?"

*　　　*　　　*　　　*　　　*

The next day Roger had been very drunk, but quiet and good. He stayed cosily in his room with the whisky and Hester stayed less cosily in hers with the miscarriage. Nanny ran up and down to her with a tight expression which said plainly it was all nonsense. She told my mother that it was very bad for Mrs. Hubert to lie in bed, she would get constipated. Nanny had always refused to give Hester her rightful title—this was another sore trial to Hester, who liked the things of this world as much as the next regular church-goer, but she pretended not to mind. "Isn't Nanny funny, she just can't work it out."

Hubert was off spreading muck on the new grass with a highly complicated machine. He took me down to look at it, and his face shone with pleasure like a child's as he pulled levers and pushed buttons.

"See—it saves two men's wages," he jolted happily backwards and forwards across the field and, sure enough, the muck was beautifully spread and the grass would take nourishment from it, and the foals would take nourishment from the grass, and when they strode as shining yearlings around the ring at Ballsbridge and made high prices it would be partly because of Hubert's Cheyne-Rice automatic-sifting reverse-action muck-spreader. My heart softened towards Hubert, for how could he hope to understand what was the matter with Roger?

And obviously, if you didn't understand, it was very tiresome and upsetting to what Hubert liked to think of as a normal household.

My heart softened so much that I even went in to see Hester.

Hester was sitting up in bed in a pink woollen bed-jacket, under which was pink nightgown and a hint of what, in Hester, could only be described as bust. She drew the bed-jacket tightly together as I came into the room. Her fair hair shone, her blue eyes were large and brilliant, her face pink and white. She was really very beautiful and unattractive.

"Do sit down, Anthony." I sat down on the edge of the bed and she backed slightly. Her attitude clearly was that you never knew with theatre people.

"How are you feeling now, Hester?"

"Oh, much better, thank you. It was just the shock, you know."

"What shock?" My hackles, in spite of myself, were rising again,

"Why, Roger, of course." She gazed pleadingly at me. "Oh, Anthony, what is to be done about Roger?"

Oh, no, you don't, my girl, I thought. Whose side do you think I'm on?

"How do you mean, Hester?"

"Well—he can't just go on like this, can he?"

"Why not? He's as happy as he'll ever be anywhere and he doesn't do any harm."

"Nor any good."

"There are a lot of people in this world who don't do any good. As a matter of fact I think Roger does more than most people."

"Oh!" She looked at me angrily. "Why can't he see a psychiatrist?"

"He did once. He was miserable for months. I know it's fashionable nowadays to rush to them as if they were deities—but they've had childhoods too, you know."

Hester looked at me in blank irritation.

"It's dreadful the way you all defend Roger, whatever he does."

"What does he do, except get drunk?"

"Isn't that bad enough?"

"God looks after children and drunks, they say, you know. Shouldn't we follow His example?"

"Anthony, please don't be blasphemous."

Hester was really angry. God was her prerogative in argument.

"Blasphemous?"

"For you to speak of God," she cried boldly, with her blue eyes flashing.

"Oh," I said.

"You, with your women and ——"

"I'm sure its very bad for you to get excited," I said soothingly. "Let's talk about something else." I picked up the book she had laid down. "What are you reading?" It was a Peter Cheyney which Andrew had lent her. It took her a good quarter of an hour to explain its social significance to me.

"I really do find it extraordinarily interesting."

"I'm sure you do," I said, and we parted friends.

*   *   *   *   *

On Saturday night Gillian and I mixed ourselves Martinis before dinner in a restive and rather gloomy manner. Nobody else was yet down. Roger was going to make an appearance at dinner—his first since the evening of the hunt. Gillian and I had been in to see him on our way down and found him muttering angrily to himself and having trouble with his tie. He looked ill and harassed.

"Hubert says I used bad language to Mama—did I?"

"No."

"And anyway," Gillian said, "just think of Hubert's language—muck-spreading and udders and contagious abortion, just all the time."

Roger gave an unwilling snort of laughter.

"You two must be down first and support me."

So we went.

Gillian examined herself in a dissatisfied manner in the glass over the mantelpiece. She was wearing a rather nice white sheath-like dress with a plain round neck and a narrow gold belt.

"I don't think I like myself in this frock."

"Why not?"

"It makes me look so experienced."

"Do you think you're going to make yourself look inexperienced by running up a little gingham number on Nanny's sewing-machine? Be your age, sweet."

"Oh, dear, I'm afraid that that's just what I *very* much am this evening."

"What's the matter?"

But I knew. I knew.

Gillian looked at herself again and trailed restively across the room to twitch at a curtain that didn't need to be twitched at. Then she trailed back to take her drink from me.

"Anthony——"

"You don't have to tell me," I said.

I was astonished and dismayed by my feelings, which were non-existent. There was a faint sense of I-have-been-here-before. Otherwise, nothing.

"Oh, God," said Gillian. "Do you mean . . . oh, you really are rather frightening at times."

"My dear—give me credit for some slight powers of observation. How else do I make my bread-and-butter?"

"Oh, God," said Gillian again. "I always mean to be so well-behaved and I seem to always turn out for the worst in the oddest way."

"It's a very common failing, let's face it," I said.

"It's lovely of you to say so, oh, darling I do assure you, nothing, nothing was further from my thoughts. It was going to be such a *relief* to marry you."

"Thank you—I rather felt the same way myself."

"But how about that lovely girl of George's?" asked Gillian, rather suddenly taking the offensive.

"Caroline."

"I'm not sure I altogether care for the way you said that, darling."

"Why should you mind, if you're going to be Roger's woman? Does Roger know, by the way?"

"Of course not. He'd never, never be so mean."

"You're rather sweet, Gillian. Are you going to marry him? You're not, I hope, dreaming of reforming him?"

"Don't, don't pretend to be stupid, Anthony. He always might reform me, of course."

"That's a very refreshing attitude, I must say. You've always been a great source of entertainment to me, darling."

"Thank you."

"Don't cry."

"I'm not."

"All right, you're not. But while Roger is reforming you, where will you live? He hasn't a penny."

"There's always my mean little alimony—perhaps your angelic Mama would like to have us in that rather revolting little back lodge that the steward won't live in."

"And in six months' time you'd be crazy for Claridge's."

"It would be warmer in the winter, certainly. Mix me another of these." She drank it very quickly and sighed and grinned. "What a hell of a lot more Hester is going to have to explain to Andrew *now*."

Caroline, I thought. Caroline. On the stony track at the foot of Sleivemore, as we headed wearily and hopefully towards where we hoped some of the quicker-witted grooms might be, the Araby little horse had begun to go short. We had dismounted and bent together to probe a dirty heel and discover where he had not quite over-reached. Caroline's hands were slender and pale, but she held his filthy hoof with absorbed tenderness.

"It's only the least touch he's given himself."

Old George and Tommy Dwyer and Gillian and Father Carrigan had clattered on, the hounds moving like ghosts around them—when we straightened up I had kissed her.

"Oh," she said in a surprised voice, after a long silence.

"Oh, what?"

"It's so strange."

"To be kissed? Ah, come now, Caroline."

"Not to be *kissed*, oh, no. But I always thought before perhaps I was peculiar."

"Peculiar?"

"To be bored—or to want to laugh."

"And you didn't then?"

"No."

"Perhaps," I said now to Gillian, "I shall take on the hounds when old George gives up."

"When you're married to your lovely girl, you mean?"

"Yes."

"I do so hope Conor won't shoot you in the back or anything. He looks to me as if he easily might."

"To me, too."

Gillian gave a shiver.

"Are we all going crazy? There's something queer about this country. What is it?"

"I don't think anybody has ever known. I think it could be—corruption."

"But darling—you love it."

"Like a fatal woman—and that doesn't mean what most people think it means. Let's snap out of this now."

"I see what you mean. It's too like Desire under the Elms. Well, to snap out of it—I'd love to know what Richmond's planning, wouldn't you?"

"I'd hate to."

"He's so very quiet—and have you noticed that whereas he started off by being a soul apart, he's become a country gentleman in the last couple of days? Have you heard him being jolly with Nanny?"

"No, thank God."

"Nanny thinks he's a very pleasant gentleman."

"I'm disappointed in Nanny. I always thought she was such a good judge of character."

"Well, but, darling, she's so right. He *is* a very pleasant gentleman—at the moment."

"I see what you mean."

*　　　*　　　*　　　*　　　*

Sitting now on the stone trough in the stable yard I thought again about Richmond. I had seen him earlier that morning leaning idly on the rails of the yearlings' paddock—a country gentleman enjoying the sun and studying the condition of his young stock. It was too damned early altogether for Richmond to be up, and when I came down to breakfast later I discovered that he had been eating porridge and sausages. There was something more than Nanny's influence at work.

Roger came back and went out again with two more of the mares. He talked nonsense to them as he went.

"Take great care of yourselves, now. One by one through the gate and no barging. Remember your conditions. I saw you rolling in a very reckless way the other day."

The mares nudged him with their heads and took little loving nips at his shoulders. Like all women, they adored him—but, unlike all women except Gillian, they had no thought of reforming him. Probably that was why they kept him more or less sane.

He came back again and went out with two more. Then two more. Then he came and took a cigarette from me. His hand still shook. He sat down beside me with a sigh.

"That Court Martial mare is going to foal before her time. I think I'll let her foal here. She's going to Little Daisy's horse and I don't much like the idea of her foaling there."

"Why not?"

"Too much dirt—too many mares—too few people." His charming, ugly face was thoughtful, tender and absorbed. Supposing I said suddenly, "Gillian won't marry me because she's in love with you?" But I didn't. I said:

"Let's walk up through the wood and sit on one of Aunt Emmy's schooling banks and look at Tipperary."

He gave me a suspicious glance.

"Are you planning to lecture me?"

"Don't be a bigger bloody fool than you can help."

He laughed. "*That* would be difficult. Come on then, while we can still see Tipperary. It's going to rain. See the sky coming down on us?"

Chapter Ten

"**I** can't think why you don't dress up like that more often," said Gillian. "You both look like the answer to the most demanding maiden's prayer—you gorgeous beasts you."

She was referring to our Hunt coats, into which we had struggled in order to dine with old George before the Hunt Ball, which this year was to be held at old George's place, Herbertstown House. There were only four houses in the West Tipperary country big enough for this function, and it was shifted year by year from one to the other as each unfortunate owner decided that really they couldn't stand it again, they'd rather move to a bungalow; than again have Paddy Casey stubbing out his cigarettes on the stair tapestry—"it would be the only one, of course, that's worth anything"—than again to have the smallest housemaid in hysterics because she had seen something nasty in the woodshed—"but there really was *no need* for her to have gone into *any* of the bedrooms"—or again to have private feuds worked out on the parked cars in the yard, so that just when you hoped at last that people might be beginning to go, just when you had said goodbye to people whom you hoped, at that moment, never to see again, you saw them again almost immediately, angrily and incoherently telephoning for the Guards.

"You look divine, both of you," said Gillian again.

"You must tell Hubert that too, when he comes down," said Roger. "Sometimes I think he feels a little out of things."

"Nonsense, darling. He just doesn't know that there are things to be in."

"Perhaps you're right," said Roger, and sniffed gloomily at his drink.

"What on earth *is* that, Roger?"

"Tonic water."

"And what?"

"And water."

"*It's not* true."

"Taste, if you like."

Gillian tasted.

"Ugh! Oh, dear, darling, what a lot of fun you're not going to have."

"I shall have tremendous fun. I shall be indulging all the evening in the very, very unusual sensation of feeling superior. And just think how I shall enjoy putting you all to bed. As smug as hell, I'll be."

"How beastly you are. Just don't bother to undress *me*, that's all. Not if you're going to be as smug as you say. I'd like to feel, at least, that you were enjoying yourself."

Roger grinned.

Hubert came in. He looked spruce, almost elegant. Only his face clashed slightly with his coat and spoilt the general effect.

"Hubert, darling, I can't tell you what a thrill you give me, in those clothes."

"These?" said Hubert. "They're very old." He looked down his nose and smiled shyly.

"You ought to wear them all the time."

"They'd get very dirty."

"Oh, but you wouldn't do any work. You'd stand on the front steps, welcoming people."

"It would look odd."

"Give Hubert a drink, darling," said Gillian hastily to me. "Is Hester not coming?"

"No. She doesn't feel quite up to it."

"I don't blame her," I said. "Who does? One really needs to go into training for a month or so."

"I'll go and kiss her goodbye," said Roger. He put down his tonic water, with relief. Gillian watched him cross to the door. She has a bad dose of it, I thought. God help her.

Richmond came in more soberly clad, most exquisite, handsome, serious, quiet. All our scarlet and white and blue silk facings paled before him. Why expect him, after all, I thought, to have a soul? Surely a body like that is enough for anyone. He walked easily over to Gillian, and told her she looked beautiful, and kissed her hand without looking silly.

"You see?" said Gillian to me triumphantly. "Some men have manners—some haven't."

"You know perfectly well that only Richmond can do that naturally, because he's an actor. If I did it, I should look as if I was acting."

"He's subtle, isn't he, Richmond?"

Richmond smiled tolerantly at me, as if I was a rather clever child. He was watching the door.

Aunt Emmy rolled in gaily, with a shining party face. Gillian had sternly helped her to dress, and the woollen garment, if present, was neatly invisible. Her fluffy, grey-blonde hair had been given a straight parting and combed the way it wanted to go, for once, and she had not been allowed to wear ribbed wool stockings, or her amber necklace, or to keep two cigars literally up her sleeve, or to tuck one of Hubert's handkerchiefs into her knickers, or to use a surcingle when she found she had lost the sash of her dress, or to just nip out, once she was dressed, to see if Micky had remembered the antiphlogistine for the roan mare's knee.

She told us all this happily, now, wrinkling her nose at the very dry Martini with which Richmond presented her. Her new black velvet dress actually was a dress for a ball —I saw Gillian's hand here again—and her white shoulders rose out of it magnificently. The face above them was sadly weatherbeaten, but who could carp at that when it beamed so with enjoyment?

"Gillian took me beads away, Anthony, she won't let me wear them, but I've put them in me bag. They're lucky. I'd never go without them."

"Oh, Aunt Emmy, honey, you've just made that up, this minute."

"They're lucky, I tell you. Haven't I worn them for thirty years?"

"Aunt Emmy, are you planning to put them on in the lavatory? I'll never, never forgive you if you do."

"I've cigars in me bag, too," said Aunt Emmy triumphantly, begging the question.

"You can't have, darling, there wouldn't be room."

Aunt Emmy looked secretive and defensive and sought hurriedly about for another topic of conversation. But Gillian pounced.

"Aunt Emmy—show me your bag."

"I left it upstairs. Doesn't Anthony look nice?"

"Aunt Emmy—is it the bag I lent you?"

"Oh now, Gillian, sure, haven't you bullied me enough? Isn't that a lovely dress you're wearing, now?"

"Or is it your knitting-bag?"

"I'm very fond of me knitting-bag," wailed Aunt Emmy.

"All the more reason why you shouldn't take it to the Hunt Ball. Think now, Aunt Emmy, darling," said Gillian cunningly, "how upset you'd be if you lost it. Everybody always loses everything at hunt balls."

"*Everything*," said Roger, who had just re-entered. He winked at Hubert, in case he was feeling out of things. Hubert, uncertain whether or not to indulge him by winking back, compromised with a non-committal nod.

*   *   *   *   *

"Hunt balls," said old George bitterly. "Balls is right. Sorry Sophia," he added belatedly to my mother, who was sitting next to him.

"Dear George, you know you're going to enjoy it almost more than anybody else. Last year you were the last to leave—nobody could get you away."

"Couldn't walk," said old George. "Gout," he added sharply, glaring down the table at Caroline, who had made a slight gurgling sound.

"Isn't he divine?" said Caroline happily to me. "I'm sure nobody ever before has had quite such a father."

"Or quite such a daughter," said Mike Harrington, bowing unnecessarily low over the table. Jane looked rather nervously sideways at him from her seat on old George's left. When we had been drinking cocktails before dinner Jane had said to me, "Anthony, darling, do please help me keep an eye on Mike—Dr. Herlihy said *no* alcohol for at least a month, and I know he's dead right because Mike had half a glass of sherry before luncheon yesterday and then made a heavy pass at Euphemia Coke—which just *shows*, doesn't it?"

Gravely I had agreed that it did, certainly, for Mike generally demanded a high standard of nubility at which to make a pass, however light.

He now looked suspiciously up the table at Jane, who was whispering to old George's butler, and turned aggressively sideways in his seat ready to trap the old b——if he tried to by-pass him. Jane signalled frantically to me with her exquisite eyebrows.

"How's the horse, Mike? I asked. "Are you going to put him into training again?"

Mike rose at once to the bait.

"*Training?* Why in hell should I put him into training? He'll make a grand hunter once he settles."

"Never over this country."

Mike returned squarely to the table, planted both elbows on it, advanced his face towards me, drew a deep breath and began to tell me exactly how good he would be over this country. Old George's butler tiptoed behind him with the champagne and Jane relaxed.

* * * * *

Hubert and Colonel Wilbraham were having a long, involved, happy argument about artificial fertilisers versus farmyard manure, colloquially referred to as muck. Utterly oblivious of their surroundings and of any duty owed to their female neighbours, they ploughed happily on.

"And where will you *get* your muck, Sir Hubert? Eh? Where will you ever get *enough*? Tell me that, now?"

"Bullocks wintered in yards," said Hubert briefly.

"But however many bullocks you have, and however much——" here he caught his wife's eye—"that is to say, *however well they work*," he bawled triumphantly, "you'll never never get enough of the damned stuff. You'll *have to resort to artificials* in the end."

Caroline looked at me and gurgled helplessly. In her capacity as hostess she had twice tried to break up this conversation, and draw the participants' attention to their social duties. They had brushed her off as if she had been an annoying insect, and returned to their enthralling muttons.

"Oh, dear, Anthony."

"Never mind, they couldn't be happier."

"But such an oasis, they're making."

"More of a desert, really. Oasis indicates an attractive lushness that is lacking."

"You're a lovely girl," said Mike loudly and suddenly to Caroline. Jane's right eye slid anxiously round, while her left one continued to enslave old George. Mike still hadn't managed to trap the champagne but his drink before dinner was not yet cold.

"Thank you, Mike," said Caroline with charming seriousness.

Mike was right. It was clever of her to wear black. Her skin had the rosy glow under the cream that enabled her to do so, and look younger than ever, and yet hint at something more than youth. Her lower lip was very full and red. She turned towards me, and the white-gold hair flopped on her creamy neck.

"I don't think you ought to hunt," I said.

"Good heavens, why not?"

"Your skin. Perishable goods. Fragile. Handle with care."

"Oh, but I plaster myself all over with grease like a Channel swimmer."

"I never noticed it," I said.

The charming, uncontrolled pink rose in her face. She picked up her glass.

Conor Molloy had abruptly broken off explaining the principles of riding a finish to Gillian and was looking at us, crumbling his toast, his dark face cold and inimical. Meeting his eye, I wondered quite seriously if he really would shoot me in the back. Gillian pursed her lips at me in a soundless whistle. And Jane had missed nothing.

*　　*　　*　　*　　*

Mrs. Wilbraham was having an alarming conversation with That Mrs. Harrington. ("Very, very smart, of course, but do you think, really . . . ?") For some reason, they seemed suddenly to be talking about the sales, and as this meant Newmarket to Jane, and Oxford Street after Christmas to Mrs. Wilbraham, it took them some time to get straightened out. When they did, at last, Mrs. Wilbraham was left with a faint feeling of chagrin, and began to talk very vivaciously to Roger about Switzerland.

*　　*　　*　　*　　*

Old George wanted to buy Aunt Emmy's little grey horse.

"Oh, come on now, do, Emmy darlin'. Tell you what, I'll even swop you my Cottage horse for him. There's an offer, now. Snap it up quick, there's a wise girl, before I think better of it."

"But George, I don't *want* to swop him for anything. He's my very best hunter, and Anthony's going to win the Hunt race on him next month."

"*Are you*, Anthony?" bawled old George down the table at me.

"Certainly not. Aunt Emmy, if you keep pledging my credit like this I shall have to put a notice in *The Times*."

"There you are, Emmy darlin'. Anthony thinks nothing of him."

"I happen to know, George, that your Cottage horse isn't sound."

Checkmated, they glared happily at each other.

*　　*　　*　　*　　*

Much later, I was dancing with Gillian.

"Have you seen Little Daisy? She's wearing blue taffeta."

"Caroline tells me she's a very nice woman."

"Of course she is—all very nice women wear blue taffeta. Will you promise to dance with her, and tell me about it afterwards?"

"What a malicious piece you are."

"I always get very, very malicious at hunt balls."

*　　*　　*　　*　　*

"What's the time? It must be fairly late—Paddy Casey is getting rowdy, and Poodle is having a crying jag."

"Oh, *where*? I must see."

"I don't think you'd be welcome—the Pytchley has the situation in hand."

"What about the Limerick?"

"Down the course, at the moment."

*   *   *   *   *

"Your tonic water smells exactly like champagne, Roger."

"Isn't it p-peculiar?"

*   *   *   *   *

"Darling, I *really* believe I'll have to take Mike home, he's behaving so oddly. He's just asked Mrs. Wilbraham to marry him."

"And is she going to?"

"She's talking it over with the Colonel, I think. Mike says she accepted."

*   *   *   *   *

"Aren't all old George's fire buckets gay? He says he will personally murder anybody who puts any cigarette ends anywhere else but in them."

"That's the death sentence, then, for Paddy Casey and me."

*   *   *   *   *

Jane had given Mike up, and was dancing with Andrew. "If you should see him actually pass out, Anthony, just tap me on the shoulder, will you?"

"I will, Jane. At the moment he's asking Poodle to go to Madeira with him."

"The ghastly thing is, she *will*."

*   *   *   *   *

Conor Molloy danced endlessly and ruthlessly with Caroline, and took her in and out to supper, and accompanied her scowling, whenever she left the floor.

*   *   *   *   *

Old George was getting confidential with my mother. "Fact is, Sophia, me wife understood me too well." "Dear George, how very tiresome and tactless of her."

*   *   *   *   *

"Gillian, I think you must speak to your son." "Oh, my dear, what's happened?" "Nothing has happened—yet. But I rather think he's planning to tell Mike that Jane is too good for him." "For who?" "For Mike, dear fool." "*Seriously*, do you mean?" "*Very* seriously." "Oh, dear, doesn't it make one feel old?"

*   *   *   *   *

At last I was dancing with Caroline. "Where's your *cavaliere-servente*? Has Nature, red in tooth and claw, forced him to leave you for a moment?" Caroline gurgled.

*   *   *   *   *

The music grew very loud, hurting my head, blurred, faded, grew loud again. Where in hell am I, I thought, and what *is* happening? Somebody had given me brandy to drink, and I hated brandy, except after dinner—but perhaps it was after dinner . . . Old George's butler . . .

Mike. . . . I opened my eyes, very surprised to find they had been shut, and saw row upon row of handsome books.

"Better?" said Roger. He and Jane were looking down at me, alarmed and amused. I swam sickly into full consciousness. I was in old George's library. "*What* the hell's going on?"

"You hit Conor Molloy, darling."

"*I* hit *him*?"

"Well, but then, of course, he hit you."

"But why? What happened?"

"Well, I don't quite know, but Conor suddenly appeared while you were dancing with Caroline and pulled her away—very rudely, I *must* say, just as if she was a tasty bone—so you hit him, very naturally."

"W-wonderful, it was," said Roger, and sat down rather suddenly on the sofa beside me. "And, owing to the great health-giving properties of t-tonic water, I was able to carry you in here."

"And I've burnt feathers under your nose, darling," said Jane. "It's a thing I've always wanted to do."

"I'm glad you've both enjoyed yourself so much," I said sourly. My head was aching abominably, my knuckles were sore, and I had made a fool of myself. I remembered now. I remembered dancing with Caroline, and then Conor's hand on her shoulder, and the way he had pulled her round to face him. I remembered the exquisite surrender to the heady rush of anger through my blood and I remembered, with a certain amount of satisfaction, what Conor's nose had looked like.

"Where's that bastard now?"

"Darling Anthony, do, *do* try and keep a tiny grip on civilization." Jane was delighted with the situation.

"He's lying down somewhere," said Roger. "And Poodle is putting ice down his back—his nose won't stop bleeding."

"Good," I said. "Where's Caroline?"

"Here," said Caroline, unexpectedly, from behind me.

"Then let's go on dancing, shall we?"

"Hadn't you better sit quiet for a few minutes?"

"No."

"My hero," said Jane, who was almost speechless with satisfaction.

I gave her a cold look, and led Caroline off. Somewhere, a long way off to one side, another Anthony Kavanagh was bent double with laughter.

*　　*　　*　　*　　*

"Your poor face looks very painful," said my mother. "And I really think, darling, you must come and apologise to George."

"I was going to, of course, and my face isn't painful a bit." But it was.

*　　*　　*　　*　　*

"Never liked the feller myself," said old George. "Can't think what Caroline sees in him. Now, Sophia, darlin', catch hold. I've told those fellers to play a decent waltz."

*　　*　　*　　*　　*

Richmond and Aunt Emmy twirled brilliantly together, swooped and turned and swooped again. Aunt Emmy beamed gaily over his shoulder at us as we passed.

"Just like riding a blood horse," she called happily

"Isn't she an angel?" said Caroline.

Gillian was dancing with Roger—or rather, moving him cautiously up and down the room like a small sailing boat tacking into a very stiff breeze.

"Promise me that you'll let me know if you feel like falling down? Because I'm smaller than you."

"Naturally I shall let you know," said Roger with dignity.

*   *   *   *   *

Much later still my mother approached me with a mild look of worry.

"Darling, if you don't particularly want kippers and coffee I think we might as well go home now—Richmond has put his knee out, poor thing. Or rather, Paddy Casey did it."

"On purpose?"

"No, I don't think so. But you know how wild Paddy gets about this time, and he suddenly wanted to show Richmond something a wrestler had taught him."

"Oh," said Gillian, "I adore Paddy—he's so original."

"Do you want kippers, Gillian?"

"No," she said sickly. "Neither does Roger, I'm *quite* sure."

We winkled out Hubert who was sitting in the library with Colonel Wilbraham talking about liver-fluke in sheep. He said it was 'straordinary how sleepy he felt. Richmond, hurriedly strapped up by a small, wild doctor who wanted to get back to bursting balloons with his cigarette ("nip out to me, now, tomorrow, and I'll slap on a bit o' plaster for you"), hopped between us, sweating, to the car, where we found Poodle and Mike, apparently imagining that they were in Madeira.

"Would you mind moving, darling," Gillian said tartly to Poodle, "into your own lovely Bentley?"

By the time we had got them out and Roger and Richmond in, the moon was fading, cold and pale, over a light, pearly frost. Depression, black and heavy, came down suddenly upon me like a thundercloud. My head was throbbing like a guitar, partly from champagne, partly from the effects of Conor's fist. I drove the big Ford sullenly and badly through the waking morning, my thoughts on the ultimate heaven of Alka-Seltzer and bed and oblivion.

"Do you know, darling?"

"What?" I snarled.

"You've absolutely promised Aunt Emmy, in the most sacred way, to ride the grey in the Hunt race."

"Witnesses, too," said Aunt Emmy in happy triumph.

"It's not ethical to hold people to promises made at hunt balls."

"I don't know what that word means," said Aunt Emmy, unmoved.

*   *   *   *   *

I idled happily down the back avenue at Knockmoree, the roan mare limping beside me, also idle and happy, stopping abruptly now and then to snatch opportunely at attractive tufts of grass. She had had a big knee since the day of the Drumanagh run, when she had indulged in her fatal little habit of not rising at her walls, and was led out ever day for the sake of her health. This was a very pleasant chore, combining as it did the feeling of

171

doing something and nothing. The day was soft, the sky blue, the earth steamy after rain, and snowdrops were appearing gallantly. Cigarette smoke hung about my head and there was not the slightest need to think about anything. We would stroll a little way up the road and look at the view, and then stroll back again and the roan mare could take some delicious nips of ivy off the high, old demesne wall as we went. We came idly to the lodge and sniffed at the turf smoke, and the mare curtseyed to the terrier who ran at us, yapping insults. Then she skittered and threw up her head, as Gillian appeared suddenly, racing wildly down the drive behind us, waving her arms. She slid to a halt, and the mare eyed her in alarm and blew indignantly. I felt rather indignant myself, thus to have my morning dreaming shattered.

"What *is* the matter, Gillian? Is the house on fire?"

"Much, much worse," she panted. Her face was really quite white.

"Hester dropped the child?"

"Don't be coarse. Far worse."

"Nothing *very* bad could happen on a morning like this."

"Any writer ought to know that it's exactly the sort of morning that the very worst things happen on. And it's happened, let me tell you." She drew a deep breath.

"Well, then?"

"Richmond is going to marry Aunt Emmy."

I remained calm. It was so utterly fantastic that it simply, obviously, was just not true.

"Since when?"

"He asked her when they were waltzing together last night—oh, the romantic *hound*—and she's accepted him and they're going to live happily ever after on a little stud farm and breed a National winner, because he's bored with the stage—so dreadfully artificial, you know—and only really likes country life. Oh, *why*, Anthony, did you ever let him come here?"

"Does my mother know about this?"

"Yes, and I really think she's pleased. They're all like Nanny; they think he's a very pleasant gentleman. Oh, I can't bear it—can we forbid the banns?"

"We must stop it somehow. Is Richmond serious?"

"For the moment, certainly. And by the time it's *not* the moment it will be too late."

I realised suddenly, with a physical sinking sensation, that Richmond *could* be serious. It was not quite so fantastic as I had supposed. His great success on the stage was not so much due to true acting ability—although he had, naturally, a certain amount of it—but in part to his wonderful looks and sexual magnetism, and in part to the fact that I knew exactly what he could play, and wrote it for him. Richmond might have been a better actor and I a better playwright if we had never met, but we made a lot of money. Yet Richmond was, in spite of his youthful appearance, nearly fifty, and very soon he was bound to start slipping, since he had neither the inclination—for he was a very vain man—nor the ability to play less glamorous parts. Was Aunt Emmy—kind, delightful, innocent, and whole-minded Aunt Emmy, to be the getting-out stakes for Richmond; to be the means of him leaning endlessly on rails staring in noble ignorance at yearlings and playing at being a pleasant and landed gentleman?

"It will be just like Marie Antoinette's dairy farm,"

said Gillian, who had obviously been following the same line of thought. "You must *do* something, Anthony." She stared tragically at me. "It's this country. It's queer, I tell you. We're all bewitched, that's what it is, I'm sure."

Chapter Eleven

Here I am, I thought—if indeed, this *is* me. It was like that moment in a recurring nightmare when you recognise what is happening to you, and realise, with an awful feeling of finality, that there is a long, nasty piece still to be gone through before you wake up. The nightmare now was that I was sitting on the front seat of the big Ford between Roger and Gillian as it ground and lurched its way through the slithery, pitted gateway into the car-park of the West Tipperary point-to-point course, and the long, nasty piece still to be gone through was due to the fact that I was finally and hopelessly pledged to ride Aunt Emmy's little grey horse in the Hunt race—which was why I was now sitting between Roger and Gillian; semi-dressed like a jockey and feeling like a mountebank, nursing a shabby racing saddle and a weight-cloth on my cold knees. The day, too, was cold; sunny, but with a nipping wind—"Going will be perfect," said Aunt Emmy happily.

The day before, I had walked the course with Aunt Emmy— indulging in hearty chat with other miserable victims of that much over-rated pastime; standing on the lips of black ditches and gazing miserably at the cold stone faces of up-banks; standing on the tops of down-banks that seemed reminiscent of Beachy Head; inspecting "the double" and "the water" and the two rather comforting low stone walls—"Only mind, now, Anthony, that you wouldn't let him think too little of them altogether—it's always the small ones that bring the falls."

Matty had been walking round with us, and had been far from re-assuring—he had said that the double put the heart crosswise in him and the first fence was not a place for Christians at all—I wondered if my leaning towards paganism would be expected to help there. Certainly, the first fence, which was one of the stone-faced up-banks with a ditch to you, was going to be tricky, for there was a very large entry of fifteen for the Hunt race, and the fence was not wide enough for more than eight horses—"You'll need to jump him off in front, Mr. Anthony, or you'll get cot." But all I had been thinking of was whether the grey horse would jump *me* off—it was delightful to find that Matty seemed to be thinking of me as a competent jockey, summing up my field at a glance, and taking quick, clever decisions. I thought how J. J. Connors had once told me that you couldn't begin to call yourself a jockey unless you knew at every second during a race exactly how each horse was going—I thought it very unlikely that I should know even how my own horse was going. Fifteen years before I had ridden, and even won, over this course, and over many others like it in Ireland; but between then and now another life, another world, stretched implacably—why, oh why, had I ever indulged Aunt Emmy? "The trouble with you, Anthony," someone had once said to me (Had she been called Maria? Yes. Suddenly and vividly, as I stared at the first fence, I saw her brown face, and the snow-goggles pushed up on her forehead.)—"The trouble with you, Anthony, is that you are weak and reckless at the same time, and that's a very dangerous combination."

Well, she was right, and look where it had landed me—right into the Hunt race on Aunt Emmy's grey horse. But not, thank God for a small crumb of comfort, into the Maiden race on the chestnut filly, for even Aunt Emmy's bouyant optimism had failed here, for once; even Aunt Emmy had been forced to admit that the chestnut filly needed a little more time, and the Kilmoganny Harriers' meeting in May would suit her better.

("But, sure, you'll be here still, Anthony."

"I will not, then.")

Old George and the Secretary and a crowd of eager underlings were here and there over the course, putting up flags and taking down wire. Caroline had been there too, muffled in an enormous fisherman's jersey and corduroy trousers, removing stones from the take-off and landing of the walls. She and old George were furious with each other, because old George had refused to allow her to have a ride round.

"And honestly, Anthony, you could strap a new-born babe onto that little horse of mine, and he'd give it a good ride."

"You shouldn't be so active," I had said. "You don't need to be an out-door girl. I'd hate you to get one of those tough point-to-point faces."

"Conor is riding in your race," said Caroline.

"I know. Presumably he'll win it easily."

"I think your grey will give him a good race," said Caroline, bending low over her task.

I looked round. Aunt Emmy and Matty had wandered on.

"Would you like him to, darling?"

Caroline came up, pink.

"Oh, Anthony, do, *do* be careful, won't you?"

"I shall probably be taken very ill just before the race."

Aunt Emmy had beckoned me on with her shooting stick, standing four-square on the slope of the ground towards the double, in her own gum-boots and my duffle-coat. "Look, Anthony, this is where you'll need to take a pull, coming down into this." Oh, lucky Aunt Emmy, to speak so glibly of taking a pull, and not having to do it herself—for would I be able to *get* a pull, with fifteen fit and excited horses galloping down hill?

"I'll do my best, you brutal woman—now let's go quietly home."

I had, even then, somehow never really believed that it was actually going to happen; but now I sat between Roger and Gillian, and looked at the race-card that had been thrust through the window of the car in exchange for half-a-crown—there was Aunt Emmy's name, and the little grey horse's name (I had never known before what it was—he seemed to be called Cloncallow), there was his age, and the weight he was going to carry, and the colours that I was wearing under my British warm.

"Oh, Lord," I said.

"Do you feel terrible?" asked Gillian.

"Squirrels."

"A tiny drop of port and brandy?"

"A big dose of it."

"Is it worse than a first night?"

"Much, much worse—after all, I don't have to be on the stage myself at first nights."

"You may be glad of that," said Richmond from the

back of the car, where he was being allowed plenty of room for his leg. "The *times* I've been sick in my dressing-room. But never again."

Aunt Emmy beamed cheerily at him and Gillian stamped angrily on the brake and the car skidded to a halt, along-side an ancient Jaguar that belonged to Euphemia Coke.

"And look—I ask you—at Little Daisy."

Little Daisy was all steeplechase jockeys rolled into one. With the peak of a stained silk cap turned up above her crash helmet, hunched professionally into her overcoat, she sat on the luggage-carrier of the Jaguar and took enormous bites at a ham sandwich, while her husband pattered anxiously about counting pieces of lead.

"Do you realise, Anthony, that she's in your race?"

"Everybody's in my race," I said, sourly.

"Never mind," said Roger soothingly. "We'll have a delicious drink now, and then we'll go and see the maidens in the paddock."

"How fascinating and unusual it sounds, doesn't it?" said Gillian. "But it's really not what you'd think at all," she added over her shoulder to Richmond, who frowned coldly at her, since he was firmly in his role of pleasant gentleman, and did not care to have racing terms explained to him in this way.

We bundled out of the warm car into the nipping wind and the bright, blowing air, and the squirrels ran round and round and jumped heavily from branch to branch in my stomach.

"I think they're *flying* squirrels," I said to Gillian.

"Oh dear, you do look a touch green, darling. Swallow this down quickly."

I sipped cautiously at the port and brandy, hating

Euphemia Coke and her great ham sandwich. But soon a warming glow began to suffocate the squirrels, and I was able to uncoil myself slightly, and even look about at the familiar scene with a certain sensation of enjoyment. Here it all was once again, unchanged by world war; the same sights, the same sounds, the same scents. The fluttering red and white flags, dotting the grey and green and scarred brown countryside; the stream of lurching, skidding horse-boxes and trailers turning with difficulty off the road with racing engines and spinning hind wheels; the luncheon parties amongst the parked cars and the disreputable characters who announced that they were looking after the cars; the unboxed horses moving nervously round in their bright best clothing; the boys selling race-cards; the old women selling sweets and bananas; the important stewards; the worried weighroom officials; the sweet trodden grass; the fresh smell of mud; the stench of car-exhausts; the salty scent of horses; the faint sighing of wind and flap of flag; the hoarse and frantic competing of the bookmakers; the shrill voices of uncontrolled and uncontrollable children begging pennies; the faint, occasional crying of rooks. Point-to-points in Ireland differ from their English counterparts a very great deal. They are quite definitely used as schooling grounds for likely steeplechasers—most 'chaser-bred horses in Ireland start their careers in point-to-points, and some have graduated from their stone walls and "doubles" to be first past the post at Aintree. The riders, except in confined races, tend to be the same tough crowd of amateurs that regularly ride against the professionals under Irish National Hunt Rules, and horses may be prepared in professional training stables without being disqualified. This, as we leant on the sagging paddock rope and looked at the skittering maidens booing, not without reason, at the unfamiliar faces surrounding them, we saw Conor, looking much the same as he had looked at Peppardstown Park, and about to ride much the same sort of horse, belonging to old Dicky; but we also saw—and this, as Gillian remarked, was different—Euphemia Coke about to ride her Tartan four-year-old.

"Is she going to ride in *every* race? Why doesn't she get breathless?"

Roger suddenly leaned secretively between our shoulders.

"Back Poodle's horse for this one—straight from the bitch's mouth; don't say I didn't tell you." He disappeared again, busily.

"Do you suppose Roger has a slight thing for Poodle?" Gillian enquired rather wistfully.

"I'm quite sure he hasn't."

"Poodle for Roger?"

"You know as well as I do that Poodle has a slight thing for everybody. Now do stop babbling. I'm feeling twitchy, and where the hell is Aunt Emmy?"

There are two types of people who jangle the nerves before a race—one who fusses madly until you are absolutely ready an hour beforehand and also ready to drop from nervous exhaustion; and one who, like Aunt Emmy, remains calm and vague and beaming and immovable even if all the other runners are in the paddock and you don't know if your own horse has arrived on the ground. Now I saw her away over on the far side of the paddock, gazing happily at the betting, with Richmond leaning heavily on a stick beside her, grave, pleasant and distinguished, pretending that the cries of "I'll lay six to four the field—three to one bar one" meant something to him.

"Listen, Gillian," I said irritably, "will you go and grab Aunt Emmy by the belt of that perfectly frightful coat and force her down to the boxes to see if the grey has arrived, and if he has make her see that he's properly bandaged, and remind her she has to declare him for the next race, and ——"

"Who's babbling *now*?"

"Well, hell, is the horse running or isn't he? God knows *I'd* just as soon he didn't."

"All right, sweet. Squirrels bad?"

"Worse every moment. In fact, I must leave you."

"Well, I'll go and trap Aunt Emmy."

After the squirrels had been momentarily soothed I wandered gloomily back to the car to collect all my odds and ends, whip and crash helmet and weight-cloth. Here Roger was drinking whisky with Mike and Jane and Andrew.

"I got threes about Poodle's horse before the money went on," he said happily. "And now he's six-to-four on, but Richmond thinks it's against and he's plunging heavily and he'll only win about t-twopence—that'll larn him."

"Darling," said Jane to me, "you have *such* a greenish tinge it's quite frightening. Are you sure you're all right?"

"I am most certainly *not* all right, Jane, thank you very much for asking."

"Terrible feeling," said Mike comfortingly. "Used to have it myself. All right once you're up, though."

"And is your glamorous stage friend really going to

marry your sweet but untidy aunt?" enquired Jane delightedly.

"Not if I can help it. And you just hush your big mouth, Jane, for once in your useless life."

"Don't start beating your chest at *me*, darling—it's in *The Times* this morning."

"Damn!" I said to Roger, "that's Richmond's doing— Aunt Emmy would never have thought of it."

Roger put a small glass comfortingly into my hand, and I sipped slowly. An unsympathetic voice demanded over the broadcasting system that the runners for the second race should come into the paddock. The maidens were bucketing off down to the start—Little Daisy's white behind bobbed at a professional angle above her plunging four-year-old.

"She can ride," said Roger, "whatever you say."

"I didn't say anything."

Mike was focusing his glasses on the starting flags. "These things always make me dizzy—can't see a thing."

"I'm going to get weighed out," I said.

Aunt Emmy came rolling genially up with Gillian actually holding on to the belt of the perfectly frightful coat.

"There you are, Anthony; your little horse is just going into the paddock—Matty says he has the race won, he's in great form, the lovely lad."

"I'm not," I said sourly.

"They're off," said Mike suddenly, still focusing. "Can't see a thing."

"They're not, darling," said Jane. "That's Tommy clearing the course."

"Rather unsuccessfully," said Gillian. "Look at those

183

terrible little boys dancing about on the double—they'll all be killed, of course—no, there's a fierce old man after them with a big stick—oh, *look* at him laying into them."

"How can you all see so much?" asked Mike fretfully. He abandoned the glasses. "That's better," he said brightly. "Those things make everything blur."

"They shouldn't," said Andrew.

"I know they shouldn't," said Mike patiently.

"Emmy darling," said Janē, "I do congratulate you. So lovely."

"He has a great chance, I think," said Aunt Emmy. "He's very fit now."

Jane looked blank, and then folded her face behind Roger's shoulder for a second. When she came out she said, "*Not* the horse, Emmy, lovely as he is."

"They're off," said Andrew. Sure enough, the little bright figures were scattering away towards the first fence.

"Who is riding Poodle's horse, Roger?"

"The new one," said Roger. He took the glasses from Andrew and began to read the race competently in a blurred voice.

"Come along, Anthony dear," said Aunt Emmy cosily, like a jolly nurse before the operation, and she and I straggled off to the weighing room, which was a rather scruffy barn, converted for the occasion.

Here was a scene of great confusion and bustle—old George sat at a table in the corner breathing fire and brimstone over late declarations, while the Secretary tried unsuccessfully to explain something into his deaf ear—horrified members of the hunt, dressed more or less as jockeys, ran about trying to borrow pieces of lead and rings and surcingles from each other, or stood in deep depression in corners or made late, hurried darts to the Elsan. One sat in the scales and asked mournfully how he could have lost three pounds between the car and here—the scale must be wrong. A line of number-cloths hung on a string across the corner, and Caroline was handing them out.

"Number seven," she said to me. "Good luck, Anthony. Do be careful—Roger's going to put on a fiver for me."

"On whom?"

"On both of you."

"The Greeks had a word for that," I said, and went over to the scales.

As I sat in them, nursing my saddle, while a sweating clerk mumbled round me and wrote hurriedly in a book, chilly excitement ran through me in waves, starting in my stomach, running the length of my spine, and chattering my teeth. I tried to think of nothing, and thought end-lessly of the narrow first fence. Outside a low murmuring began, rose to a sustained roar, and died abruptly. Some-body had won the maiden race. As I came out of the barn Little Daisy was being led into the winner's enclosure, purple and sweating, while Conor, also sweating, and rather sulky, kicked old Dicky's horse into the second stall. Poodle's Colonel and Poodle's horse were edging unhappily towards the third place, through a definitely threatening crowd. ". . . And to do it broad-like, in the middle of a field, 'twas not right," declared an angry voice.

"What on earth's happened?" I asked Roger, who had materialised suddenly out of the crowd.

"That silly chap missed a flag out in the country when he was leading by half a field and had to go back—if you hadn't glasses it must have looked as if he'd taken a very violent pull—all the local money was on, and now I think he's going to get lynched, and Poodle's having hysterics and has sent for the Guards."

Aunt Emmy had taken my saddlery and gone off with it vaguely in the direction of the paddock. I followed forlornly, wondering if the chattering of my teeth looked as obvious as it felt.

"They've opened the betting," said Roger cheerily. "Little Daisy's horse is favourite, and Conor's is second favourite—he's riding the horse that you finished the Drumanagh run on."

"He's fast enough, anyway."

"I got fours about you—but what with Aunt Emmy and Gillian and Caroline and myself all plunging I should think you're probably favourite by now."

Here was the paddock gate, and here was Colonel Wilbraham being a steward and loving every moment of it, blooming and vociferous, chatty and welcoming to those who were entitled to be in the paddock, and reprovingly chatty to those who were not—"Now then, FitzPatrick, those ropes aren't there for you to go crawling under like that, y'know."

"Isn't that me own brother-in-law, Colonel, that's over there, leading Mr. Molloy's horse this minit, and he beckoning for me to help him."

"Why does he want help?"

"Sure, that horse is a terror to lead, and he dragging at you—even a big man like yourself, Colonel, might get a weakness from the way he'd take it out of you."

Colonel Wilbraham looked across the paddock to where Conor Molloy's horse was sidling quite obediently beside FitzPatrick's soi-disant brother-in-law.

"If he wants help, which I doubt, he can ask you when he comes round. Meanwhile, please stay behind the ropes."

"These fellers will say anything," he confided to me. "I don't suppose he's any relation at all of that other feller, and he certainly wasn't beckoning to him. Jolly tricky to keep the paddock clear when none of these fellers will tell the truth."

"Very tricky indeed," said Roger gravely. "I hope you're going to let us in?"

"Having a ride round, eh?" said the Colonel to me. "That's right. Must fill up the Hunt race. That's the stuff." His attention was distracted then by a rat-like face that came up suddenly under his elbow and begged to be allowed to cut across quick to get to the babby that was bawling beyond. "Why can't you go *round*?" demanded Colonel Wilbraham helplessly.

"And I to lose him again in the crowd before I'd get there?"

Roger gave it as his opinion as we walked to the centre of the paddock that Colonel Wilbraham would be certifiable long before the last race. "Either that, or this will be a seething mass of people looking for babies and helping their relations, because he'll have given up trying."

"Why are you here, anyway?"

"I'm going to take off your overcoat—you'll never be able to get it off yourself."

The little grey horse—officially Cloncallow, 6-12-7—walked round calmly with his long, slouching stride, looking traditionally likely to lep Aintree, with Matty, happily self-conscious, at his head. Hands reached at him out of the crowd and voices enquired if he was going to win to-day and Matty trod on air.

Conor came into the paddock looking grim and sulky. He had not relished being beaten a head by Little Daisy. He stood contemptuously apart, bending his whip into a bow between his hands.

"Nasty temper," said Roger. "You and Little Daisy had better lie up together in this."

Somebody in a neat suit was running to and fro shouting hopefully. There was a general swirl of horses towards the centre, a flapping of sheets being pulled off, a squeaking and kicking as girths were tightened. Pink and white flashed in the air, and there was Euphemia Coke up on a big, black, rather horrified horse.

"Did you see?" said Roger. "She spat on her hands." He removed my coat with the firm kindness of a surgeon. "Up you go, now."

Up I went.

The little grey horse, who had always seemed to me a very comfortable ride, felt as jerky as a clockwork toy beneath me. His neck looked snaky and wicked and he had laid his ears back as I landed in the saddle. The lead was hard beneath my knees, the reins felt enormously thick and very stiff in my cold hands, and I knew that if he so much as offered to play up, I should fall off immediately. I felt as if I had never been on a horse before, and I would have given the remaining years of my life to be able to slip quietly off him and curl up somewhere with a good book.

"Good luck now," said Roger and other voices—Aunt Emmy's and Colonel Wilbraham's—repeated it "Good luck now, good luck," and hands reached up to pat my knee, and Matty had led me out through the gate behind Little Daisy's broad white behind and her horse's broad black one, and then he had dropped his hand from the bit and said, "I'll be looking for you, now, Mr. Anthony," and I was alone in the great, cold world.

The grey horse, annoyed by my nervous tremors, grabbed irritably at his bit and shook his head. Then he plunged suddenly sideways, nearly sending me down his shoulder. Conor had jumped his horse abruptly into a canter from just behind us. He might or might not have done it on purpose, but he was grinning as he went by, and his grin had the blood drumming in my ears at once. "Darling Anthony, do, do try and keep a tiny grip on civilization." Jane's voice was very faint and far away as I sat down on the grey, feeling at last as if I had ridden horses before, and sent him along down to the start. The wind blew in my face, the sun shone, the horse strode out happily, the squirrels ceased their mad career, and warmth and confidence came back to me.

Down at the start Conor and Little Daisy circled each other like angry cats, each trying to get the berth on the extreme left, for the course was a left-handed one. Such refinements, I felt, were not for me. I let the grey stand idly on a loose rein well behind the other horses while the starter droned over his words about leaving the red flags on our right and the white flags on our left.

"And God have mercy on our souls," said Dr. Paddy Herlihy cheerfully, as the peroration came to an end. He was mounted on a rangy, nerve-racked young horse that belonged to Pat Delaney, and whose next race would probably be at Punchestown. "Are you going to win this?" I asked him.

"I might, then, only for the water. This felly has a fright of water—he'll be looking into it and smelling it the very same as if 'twas his feed before him. Don't get behind me now at it, or I might be stopping you." His horse sidled anxiously sideways and took an hysterical nip at my knee. At the same moment somebody barged into me from the other side, gasped a worried apology and bounced off again. It was the wife of a trainer from Clonard—a blonde and fluffy piece who was always being picked out of ditches hunting and who would obviously not get very far now. "There's another you'd need to stay away from," said Dr. Paddy cheerfully. "She wouldn't know where she'd be at all, once she'd be off."

It seemed to me that there was really going to be very few people it would be safe for me to be near at all. Conor was undoubtedly after my blood; Little Daisy, although, so far as I knew, free from any personal animosity towards me, was a very competent race-rider who was certainly not going to let any chances slip; and nobody else seemed really very likely to have much control over their horses. I decided that I would lie up on the outside, as far away from Conor and Little Daisy as possible, and try to go in front until the thinning-out process had been accomplished. So I pulled the grey out towards the right, and then we were all moving in an anxious, jostling, jumpy, hard-breathing line towards the equally jumpy starter— who had a right to be jumpy, for the trainer's wife's horse suddenly pounced madly out of line straight for him, swept under his horse's nose, and galloped off, pointing roughly for the paddock.

"I'd say she wouldn't be back," said Dr. Paddy, still cheerful, as we wheeled confusedly round again—but there she was, having pulled round in a circle, coming up again from behind, still at full gallop. Little Daisy's opinion of her own sex was electrifying the air around us. "Sure, we must go now, or we'll all be knocked," said Dr. Paddy. The starter seemed to be of the same opinion, for he made a feeble flapping gesture at us—barely lifting the flag before he let it fall again—and pulled smartly out of the way. Matty and Aunt Emmy had schooled the grey horse well and indefatigably, and now he jumped into his bit without hesitation, and was into his stride smoothly and quickly—but even so, out on the left, both their horses pulling double, Conor and Little Daisy were a good three lengths clear. The narrow first fence hurried towards us, the grey horse reached for it gaily, it loomed an instant and was gone, all its horrors, its dark ditch, its cold stone face, dissolved beneath one longer, lifting stride, and between the confident, cocked grey ears the first wall showed ahead, a dark bar between its gay flags. There went Conor, there went Little Daisy, green-and-gold, and pink-and-white, neither of them moving over it —Dr. Paddy's horse came racing up and jumped level with us, wildly, its head high, fighting the bit, while its imperturbable rider begged it genially to steady down, for the love of God.

Between the wall and the next fence I took a swift glance over my shoulder. There, somewhat to my surprise, was the trainer's wife, bobbing indefatigably along, rolling slightly in her saddle, but still attached to her horse; there was a pale-faced lad, said, I remembered, to be a nephew of old George's, mounted on one of the Hunt horses; and there was a red-faced lad on a horse of Paddy Casey's. There were also three loose horses, enjoying themselves madly. There must have been quite a scrimmage at the first fence.

Now we were bearing sharply left-handed, and the ground was beginning gently to slope towards the double. I drove the grey horse hard for a few strides to get clear of Dr. Paddy's horse, who was going to smell the water when he came to it, and was also, I had noticed, inclined to jump across his fences. Then I let him settle down, in third place, to the right of Conor and Little Daisy and several lengths behind them. I thought of the excited group that would now be clinging over the car like grapes on a vine, and I could see Roger reading the race—because he could do it even when he had drink taken, and nobody else could do it properly even when dead sober—putting back the whisky happily without removing the glasses from his eyes. "Conor and Little Daisy making the running—Anthony tracking them—Dr. Paddy lying up with him—and by God, there's that fluffy piece of Joey's still there."

Before me the green-and-gold, the pink-and-white, raced steadily together, straight as arrows, unvarying in pace or course, meeting their fences right every time and flicking over them with an almost insolent ease. Two down-banks, and now the double, green and humped and enormous, and looking bigger than Becher's, and the drink definitely dead in me. "This is where you'll need to take a pull, Anthony." Well, that, after all, was going to be easy. I took one, and then let him go on at it. On our right, masked in thorns and trees, was the place where Father Carrigan and Gillian and myself had jumped it during the Drumanagh run. Oh, to be there now, to steady into a gentlemanly trot—but the grey horse had no such foolish misgivings. He reached for it as boldly as ever, his ears cocked, measuring his take-off, as it loomed at us, its sacred green scarred with brown hoof-cuts where the maidens had jumped it before us, and doubly scarred there, on the left, where the shining quarters of Conor's brown horse and Little Daisy's black had heaved and risen and disappeared in front of us. The grey, timing it like a dancing-master, soared and swept and kicked back, and landed with a self-congratulatory shake of his clever head, and with thud and creak of leather Dr. Paddy landed alongside us, his puggy face glowing, and his young horse settling down at last. I saw him take a pull and disappear again behind—he was looking for a lead over the water. Now, left-handed still, we would soon begin to climb the rise behind Kilgarvan—we would go right up round it, and then, coming down towards the finish, jump the first two fences as the last two—so that the last one was a down-bank, very nasty on a tired horse jumping carelessly. But here, meanwhile, was the water, a genuine babbling stream, masked by a black little thorny hedge, through which the sun glinted off the ripples at us. And here, appearing suddenly near my right knee, and galloping with a happy intransigence that boded no good to anyone, came one of the loose horses, a big, sweaty, half-clipped chestnut with a narrow white blaze, his breast-girth broken, his saddle on his loins, and his expression betokening great interest and enjoyment. "Why don't we do this sort of thing more often?" he seemed to be enquiring genially, as he loomed alongside.

Too late to get ahead of him—too late to pull back—too late to do anything but rise together in unhappy proximity at it. A sweaty shoulder bumped my knee, a flying on cracked agonizingly across the knuckles of my right hand, the grey jumped to the left, dwelt as he landed, lurched, and bit angrily at the loose horse's quarters. In a flurry of stabbing heels, whistling whip and fearful threats, Dr. Paddy landed beside us, inelegant, but safely over. "Jesus," he said gaily, "you nearly had us stopped yourself. The loose horse strode excitedly ahead up the hill, making up ground rapidly on Conor and Little Daisy, who were coming back to us, giving their horses an easy, unaware of the trouble behind them. Dr. Paddy and I went side by side slowly and contentedly up the hill and over another wall—the loose horse, an unwelcome guest, caught the leaders and bounced happily along with them, like a bore suddenly taking charge of the conversation. And then, to my amazement, the fluffy piece of Joey's came ranging up on our left, rolling about in her saddle, but still there and still in the race, her horse going great guns and thoroughly in charge of the situation. Dr. Paddy shouted to her, in rather an unsportsmanlike fashion, that her shirt was out of her breeches, she was barely decent. But, refusing to be side-tracked, or to lose her very small reserve of breath, she looked grimly ahead and kept grimly on beside us. And now, I thought, very soon somebody is going to begin to race—and perhaps that somebody had better be me, since Conor and Little Daisy are already too far ahead. At the top of the hill, as we landed over a down-bank, round on the far side of Kilgarvan where the ground now began to slope very gradually towards the far, shining, beetly rows of the parked cars, and when we had come two-thirds of our journey of "about three miles", I asked the grey horse to go on and he responded strongly and uncomplainingly, lengthening his stride and lowering his head, with gay determination. But Conor and Little Daisy, the old hands, were not to be easily fooled. Neither had looked round, but now, almost at the same instant, both quickened and began to race as if the grey horse's move had started an electric current through the field. Over another bank we all kept the same places, all moving faster, but then I saw, with a leap of the heart, that Little Daisy's horse, at least, was coming back to me. Back and back, until the grey horse swept up and jumped level with the black, and for half a field I rode stride for stride with the hunched pink-and-white, the set jaw, the faint blonde moustache, the red hands steady and capable on the plaited reins, the poised white rump—then they dropped back by my shoulder, then they vanished, and the grey horse and I went on after Conor, still several lengths ahead, and much bothered still by the loose chestnut striding away happily on his left. As he went into the next fence he raised his whip and slashed it across the head several times, but the horse, with the misplaced affection of its kind, came right back and kept right on.

Two fences to go now, the wall and the last. Down the slope of the ground we raced, into the sun, the grey horse fully extended now, no sound in the world but the thudding of his hoof-beats and my own breathing—too loud, too laboured—no sight but the lean, stretched neck, the neat plaits of mane, the cocked grey ears, the green-and-gold jacket ahead—no sensation but the hardness of the lead beneath my knees, the aching stiffness in the small of my back, the enormous effort of scrubbing him on, on, on, in time with his swinging stride. There went Conor over the wall; the loose horse switched suddenly off to the left in gay inconsequence, scattering a blur of pinkish faces—they came back, gaped—were gone, as the wall dropped behind us, unfelt, almost unseen, and Conor looked briefly round and picked up his whip. And now, my lad, I thought, in enormous senseless exultation, I have you, I have you cold—for the brown horse was beaten, it could not pull out any more, it was swerving under the whip, and it swerved to the right. And the little grey horse, the noble Cloncallow, six years, twelve stone of exhausted live weight and seven pounds of lead, responding generously to my urgency, nipped in to take the inside berth over the last jump—a great advantage here, for on landing we had to turn sharply left-handed to go up into the straight. "Ride into the last as though it wasn't there," and we were certainly doing just that—the wind of our going blurred my eyes with tears—the murmuring of the crowd began—suddenly and clearly I heard somebody shouting the grey—and suddenly too, less clearly, out of the corner of one blurred eye I saw Conor's face—and realised, too late, the vulnerable position I had put myself in; just a head behind and on the inside. Too easy to pull across and knock me outside the turning flag—for who is to say that a tiring horse, a horse that has already swerved once, may not jump crooked at the last? And who is to be blamed? And what would Conor care, so long as I didn't win the race? Too late. We were launched together out over the ditch, our irons clashing, an agonising pressure on my right knee, the grey's ears laid suddenly flat back. Then we were crashing together, somersaulting sickeningly in a whirl of threshing hooves. Then the earth came up and smacked me jarringly in the face, and I went reeling into soundless, thoughtless oblivion.

Chapter Twelve

"Talk about Ethel M. Dell," said Gillian.

"I don't," I said coldly.

"If you could only have seen yourself—I had no idea you could look such a caveman—your eyes were those dear old gleaming slits—*frightening*."

"Your lively imagination will lead to madness some day," I said. "You should try and curb it, sweet."

"Ask Roger then. There we stood, by the last, and there you were coming into it, looking just as I say and Conor slightly worse—only very slightly—and Roger said 'My God, there's going to be dirty work here'—and then there you both were—arse over tip, at our very feet."

"You have a lovely, pure narrative style," I said.

"Horrid, it was. I was so nearly sick, you can't think. Both the horses upside-down—and the woman next to me screamed very loudly and shut her eyes and asked Roger to tell her if the boys were quinched, both. And then the horses getting up, and you and Conor both as quinched as could be—and then Little Daisy coming plugging along, so we all had to stand over you and Conor and wave madly at her to keep out to the right— she was maddened, rather naturally, because there she was, winning, and there was everybody just pouring down to look at the blood, and taking no notice of her at all—and then Dr. Paddy bursting along—he'd taken a fall at the second last and got up again, and I think he must have been a bit shook, because he took totally no notice of any of us and landed very nearly bang on top of you— perhaps he was hoping to make you a life-long patient— and then there was a little man with an enormous flag signalling hopefully for the ambulance, but the driver had won big money on the first race and was in the bar— in the end Mike brought it down—and Roger and I had hell for ages trying to stop two frightening little boys in an odd uniform from practising first aid on you—but for us, you'd certainly be dead."

"On the whole, I'm not sure that I'm grateful."

"You're very difficult to amuse, to-night. And to think that I stayed away from the ball-dancing to succour you."

"*You*'d be very difficult to amuse if you had a head like mine."

"I really feel you ought to have stayed in bed to-day."

"Balls."

"No need to be heroic, darling, surely, with your oldest girl-friend? I'll mix you a delicious drink—such a good thing you weren't concussed, that would make it all the more depressing. Poor dear Aunt Emmy—however, a good thing the horse wasn't hurt, and she'll be as happy as a bee to-night telling old George that he had the race won, even if he isn't by Cottage."

Everybody but Gillian and Richmond and myself had gone off to the Black and Tans hunt ball—even Hester had bravely ventured forth smothered in accordion pleating and assured by Hubert that no one would ever know.

"Don't let Paddy Casey start throwing you around,"

Gillian had said to her. Hester looked haughty, for she thought Paddy Casey a common little man and had never been known to dance with him. Hubert came up like an anxious sheepdog and hurried her into the car, a hand under her elbow.

"Poor darling Roger," said Gillian. "He will dance with her all night, while Hubert tells a few Colonels how to thresh linseed."

"Whatever makes you think so?" enquired Roger, coming down the stairs, once more resplendent in scarlet and dark blue.

"Because you're so foolishly kind, darling. Did you ever read a considerably depressing book called *Beware of Pity*?"

"No," said Roger. "I've only read *Chaseform* and *Raceform*, and I'm going to dance all night with Poodle, so perhaps I'd better have a big drink before I begin. Thank you. Poor Anthony, how are you feeling now? Lord, you did give the ground a smack—but Conor's worse, you'll be glad to hear. His horse rolled on him."

"The b——" I said, "I'll have him up for it."

"Now, *darling*," said Gillian, "don't, *don't* be so ferocious. Just leave things alone. Don't start things. After all, look what an enormous amount of money we owe his unspeakable old father—four hundred pounds he told me yesterday, very genially, just between friends—oh, the old beast, and I'm sure the drink was doctored."

There was an impatient toot from the car.

"Better go," said Roger. "Do I look Poodle-worthy?"

"You do indeed, darling. So much so that I must give you a small kiss before you go."

The small kiss bestowed, and Roger gone, Gillian

looked suddenly white, tired and strained. She drank the dregs of Roger's Martini in silence, and in silence chewed the olive, gazing into the fire. I felt enormously sorry for her, for myself, for everybody. My head was still buzzing from its encounter with the ground, I had a very tender, just not broken, nose and a cut lip and I could not see out of my left eye. I had also, in the classic tradition, broken my collar-bone for the third time. We sat in continued silence and heard Richmond thumping about stiffly in the room above us, and rain falling outside. The labradors stirred in a tangled, sleepy pile much too near to the fire, and the white greyhound, who had recently been dipped in Lux, posed self-consciously and most exquisitely on the forbidden sofa.

"I love this room," said Gillian sadly. There was no need to answer, and again we were silent for a long while.

Then she said, "Do you know what? Perhaps you'll think I'm getting hysterical—but I know we'd much better go away from here and take Richmond with us."

"When?" I asked.

"Now. Tonight. *This very minute*. It's our only chance. If we don't go now we'll never go—we'll never know how much is enchantment and how much is true—we'll never wake up until suddenly, one day when I'm washing Roger's socks in the back lodge, and you're watching hounds work over plough, and Richmond is walking pleasantly round the sales paddocks at Ballsbridge—suddenly, just, the spell will break and we'll say 'we were mad' and it will be too late."

She was in deadly earnest and there were tears in her eyes. I was very tired and profoundly depressed. Ever since I had come round in the ambulance with Roger telling me to take it easy and my mother's face small and worried by his shoulder, the enormous absurdity of my rivalry with Conor had begun to strike me more and more. Emotionally and physically exhausted after the heat and effort and excitement of the race I no longer felt desire for Caroline, or indeed for anybody. I would go quietly away with Gillian whose mind and body were soothing and familiar to me, who would not betray me into weakness and recklessness, who would not fuss if I was so betrayed by others. I would recuperate quietly in my civilized rooms, and presently we would quietly get married and quietly go to Spain for a bit, and when we came back I would bend Richmond to my will about the play, and the clamour of the West Tipperary foxhounds would die away.

"San Felieu de Guixols," I said.

"What?"

"That's where we'll go to, in Spain."

"Are we going to Spain?"

"In a little while, I hope."

"How are we going to get Richmond to come away from here?"

"We'll tell him that we think it absolutely necessary for Sir Harvey Brice to see his knee at once, or he may be left with a permanently stiff leg."

"Darling, you really are sometimes quite clever—of course, that's the one thing that would work."

"But Aunt Emmy," I said. "Hell, I don't know. Ought one to interfere so much in other people's lives? Presumably she *wants* to marry Richmond."

"Oh, no, she doesn't. She wants to marry a very pleasant gentleman."

"Well then—she'll be very hurt when the very pleasant gentleman suddenly makes off while she's at a hunt ball."

"How very, very much more she'll be hurt if he doesn't."

"I suppose so. I wish my head would stop aching."

"Oh, Anthony, *you* know your sweet Aunt. She has no particular feelings about Richmond, I do assure you of that. She looks upon him as an unexpected Christmas card—pleasant, but not really meaning much in one's life. She thinks it would be great fun to be a married woman—how wrong she is, the sweet thing—but once he's gone she'll just slide happily on, and think only about the new crop of foals."

"I expect you're absolutely right—and if we're going, there *is* only one way to do it, we'd better go as you say, now, this minute. My God, I'm tired. You'll have to drive."

"What in?"

"We'll take that foul little green car and leave it in the Shelbourne garage. I'll write a note now, for Mama."

"Won't she be madly surprised, not to say hurt?"

"No. It's only people like Hester who get surprised and hurt, in order to make others feel bad about surprising and hurting. Mama will be interested and sympathetic and sorry that we're missing Punchestown and hope that we won't eat twice-cooked meat in restaurants."

"Oh, the absolute heaven of your mother—but, oh dear, what shall I do about my awful child? For a moment I had almost forgotten him—am I to leave him whirling about with Jane at hunt balls?"

"I can't really feel that you have much chance of persuading him to come away while he's in this chop-licking mood."

"Wouldn't a really good mother be able to—Hester, now, for example?"

"The hypothesis is false. No child of Hester's would be whirling with or chop-licking over Jane."

"True, I suppose. Well, then, I'd better write a little note for him, and leave him a cheque. Oh, hell." She sighed heavily, half sad, half laughing. "I can't help wishing that I was leaving a little note for *you*, being about to run off with Roger."

"You were always an honest girl. Would you leave me a cheque, too?"

"Oh, no—I wouldn't be able to afford it."

We looked at each other and began to laugh.

"Shall I go up now and terrify Richmond about his permanently stiff leg?"

"Yes—have an uncle whose leg got so stiff it had to be amputated."

"Funnily enough, I did have, I believe."

"All the better then. I'll go and find Nanny and get her to pack for us."

I found Nanny busily tidying-up in my mother's room.

"Nanny, Mrs. Lodwick and Mr. Kerr and I have to go back to London quite unexpectedly."

"Yes, dear?" said Nanny unhelpfully, beady-eyed.

"Would you ever be an angel, Nanny, and pack a few things for us?"

"Most of your shirts are in the laundry dear, and the King himself would never get them out of those nuns before Saturday at the very earliest."

"The hell with my shirts, Nanny—this is urgent."

"You were always a one, Anthony, for rushing here, and rushing there, and no real reason for any of it, and please don't use those words to me, I've spoken to you before about it."

"Sorry, Nanny."

"Must you really go tonight, dear? Couldn't you just stay over? You really don't look fit to go flying off in this way—Bridget remarked to me just this minute gone that you looked really washed-out this evening. Why don't you go straight to bed and I'll bring you up something hot to drink?"

"Oh, Nanny, don't seduce me, I'm too tired."

"Well, dear, if you must go, you must, and I'll see what shirts I have in the airing cupboard. And Mrs. Lodwick's dressing-gown too, I was just mending—I might pack Roger's for her that she's been using and then she could send it back."

"No," I said. "Pack her own."

"Roger will be very disappointed to find you gone, he loves to have you here. Mrs. Hubert isn't such company for him."

"No," I said.

"And Mrs. Lodwick is very fond of him."

"Yes," I said, meeting her wise, faded eyes.

"Perhaps it's all for the best," said Nanny, in her sibyl tones. "Now don't you worry dear."

*   *   *   *   *

Luckily it was too late when we arrived at the Shelbourne for it to be full of cheery people I didn't want to talk to, all asking me what on earth I had done to my face. I was extremely irritable, and Gillian shepherded me anxiously to bed and then spent a long time ringing up Aer Lingus and leaving hopeful instructions with the night porter for being called in the morning. Richmond had ceased to be very pleasant, and was being very egotistical about his knee, and very tiresome about not having a bathroom. ("Oh, you poor sweet, but you must look such heaven in the early morning, surely you can't mind being seen?") In revenge for this rather ill-timed pleasantry Richmond suddenly attacked me violently over the play, accusing me, rightly, of having done no work on it, and, wrongly, of deliberately trying to ruin his career. He seemed quite to have forgotten Aunt Emmy. We spent a hideous night.

*   *   *   *   *

In the heavily bumping Dakota Gillian said cheerily to Richmond, "Do you ever look out along a wing and imagine that suddenly you'll see a *great crack* in it, and then the whole thing will break off and go plunging away down into space?"

"*No*," said Richmond, palely. "Of course I don't. Nor does anybody who hasn't a peculiar and morbid mind."

He opened the *Tatler* sternly, but his eyes kept sliding nervously sideways to glance out of the little round window.

Beneath us the bright and patchy fields, the white cabins, the stone walls, fled backwards and vanished. Then there was the shadow of the land under the sea. Then there was just the sea, and I could have wept. "There is a world elsewhere." But was there? At that moment, I thought not.

*   *   *   *   *

"Of course," said Gillian, screwed round in the seat she was sharing with Richmond, and whispering to me over the top of it. "We could always go back."

"Could we?"

*   *   *   *   *

We had luncheon in the Causerie at Claridge's. Richmond was petulant because Sir Harvey Brice's secretary would not give him an appointment before four o'clock. He stumped stiffly round the centre table, loaded with Smörgåsbord, and curled his nostrils superbly at this and that.

"You must admit", said Gillian, "he could look madly interesting to anybody who didn't know him." And certainly several people *were* madly interested and hissing excitedly to each other that surely that was Richmond Kerr. Richmond found this very stimulating. He put up a strong, beautiful hand and thoughtfully fingered the greying, carefully brushed-up hair above his right ear, while he studied the tunny-fish with noble gravity and gave his profile to a mutation mink.

"Shall we go and pick ourselves some goodies?" asked Gillian.

"Wait a moment. Don't let's spoil this scene."

Presently Richmond came back to our table with a loaded plate. He was much thawed. "Aren't you two going to eat anything?"

"Oh dear," said Gillian, picking away idly. "Think of Knockmoree now."

"Don't do anything so bloody stupid," I said. "Leave it. Dead."

"Oh, you're so right, I suppose."

We moved unhappily round spearing at bits and pieces

with our forks, and then I came upon two people who immediately asked me what on earth I had done to my face. For a moment I simply could not think who they were—but of course, they were called Gerry and June Somebody, and I had spent Christmas (it seemed incredible) with them. The house (in Surrey) had been an outstandingly perfect example of Stockbroker Tudor, with slight Curzon Street Spanish interior influence, but the food had been good. Now they were asking me where I would be for Easter.

"Fairyhouse," I said.

Gillian dropped her fork, with which she had just speared a pickled onion. Gerry Somebody looked slightly worried and said he was sure he knew the name, wasn't it old Fort Munro's place? No, I said, it was a racecourse where the Irish Grand National was run, not very far outside Dublin. June Somebody said How very original, rather coldly, and they left us.

"But darling," said Gillian. "Are you really going to Fairyhouse?"

"No. I just suddenly thought how pleasing it would be if I was."

"Oh, dear, *wouldn't* it be?" She dabbed unenthusiastically at some potted shrimps. "It's *so* hot in here. Do you suppose, darling, that we've done the right thing, at all?"

"How can we possibly know? How will we ever know?"

That was just the hell of it, of course. How would we?